# Magical History Tour

# Albert Einstein

**FABRICE ERRE**
Writer
**SYLVAIN SAVOIA**
Artist

PAPERCUTZ
NEW YORK

# Magical History Tour

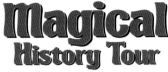

**#6 "Albert Einstein"**

By Fabrice Erre and Sylvain Savoia

Original series editors: Frédéric Niffle and Lewis Trondheim
Translation: Joseph Laredo
Lettering: Cromatik Ltd

Jordan Hillman – Editorial Intern
Jeff Whitman – Managing Editor and Production
Jim Salicrup
Editor-in-Chief

ISBN 978-1-5458-0773-6


www.papercutz.com

Papercutz books may be purchased for business or promotional use. For information on bulk purchases please contact Macmillan Corporate and Premium Sales Department at (800) 221-7945 x5442.

Printed in Malaysia
November 2021

Distributed by Macmillan
First Papercutz Printing

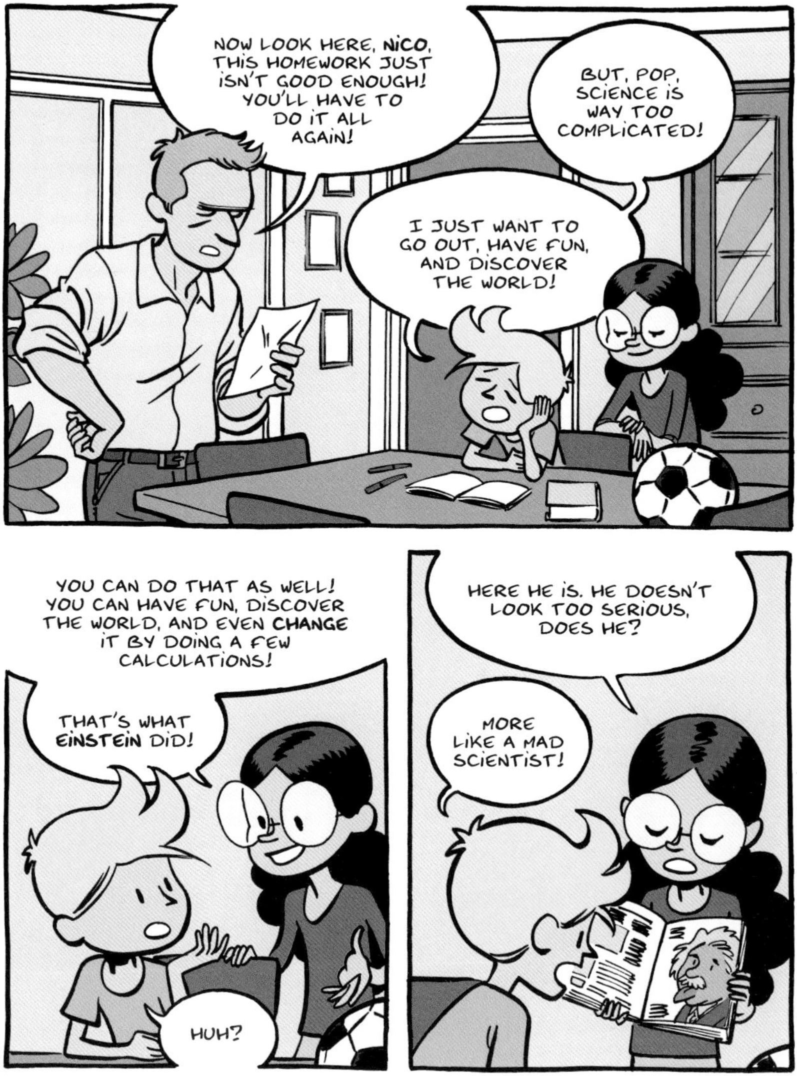
NOW LOOK HERE, **NICO**, THIS HOMEWORK JUST ISN'T GOOD ENOUGH! YOU'LL HAVE TO DO IT ALL AGAIN!
BUT, POP, SCIENCE IS WAY TOO COMPLICATED!
I JUST WANT TO GO OUT, HAVE FUN, AND DISCOVER THE WORLD!
YOU CAN DO THAT AS WELL! YOU CAN HAVE FUN, DISCOVER THE WORLD, AND EVEN **CHANGE** IT BY DOING A FEW CALCULATIONS!
THAT'S WHAT **EINSTEIN** DID!
HUH?
HERE HE IS. HE DOESN'T LOOK TOO SERIOUS, DOES HE?
MORE LIKE A MAD SCIENTIST!

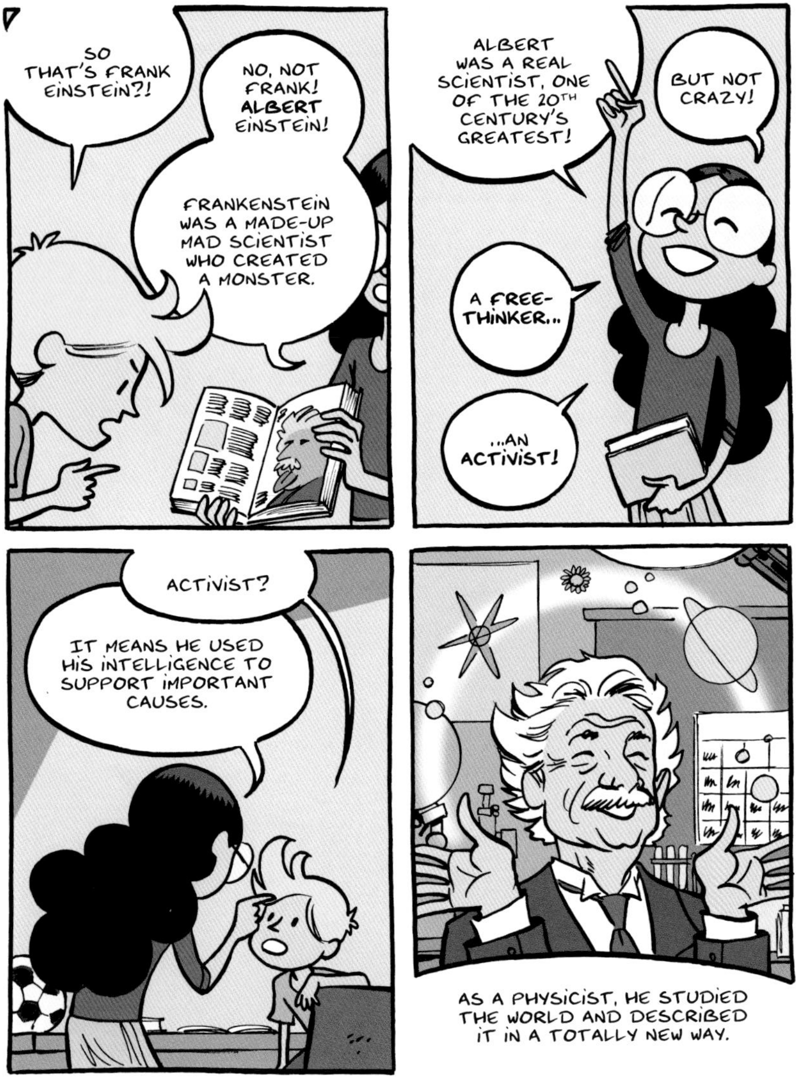
SO THAT'S FRANK EINSTEIN?!
NO, NOT FRANK! **ALBERT** EINSTEIN!
FRANKENSTEIN WAS A MADE-UP MAD SCIENTIST WHO CREATED A MONSTER.
ALBERT WAS A REAL SCIENTIST, ONE OF THE 20TH CENTURY'S GREATEST!
BUT NOT CRAZY!
A FREE-THINKER...
...AN ACTIVIST!
ACTIVIST?
IT MEANS HE USED HIS INTELLIGENCE TO SUPPORT IMPORTANT CAUSES.
AS A PHYSICIST, HE STUDIED THE WORLD AND DESCRIBED IT IN A TOTALLY NEW WAY.

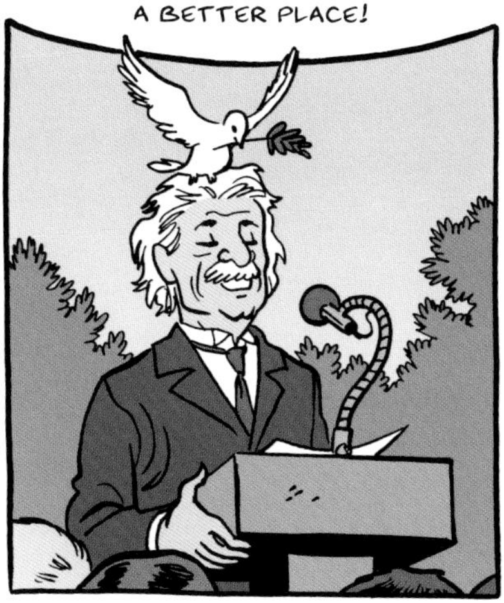
AS A PERSON, HE TRIED TO MAKE THE HUMAN WORLD A BETTER PLACE!
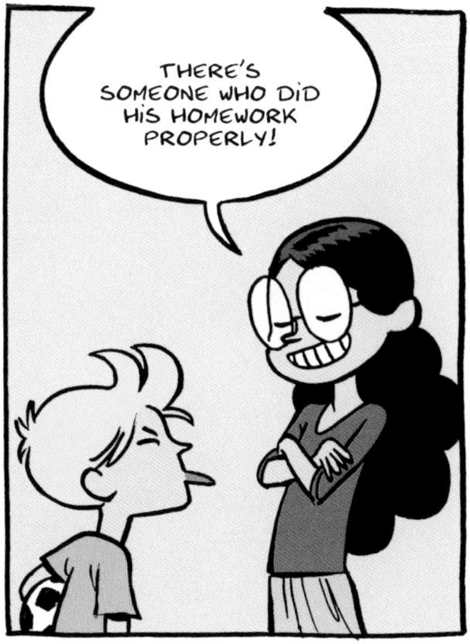
THERE'S SOMEONE WHO DID HIS HOMEWORK PROPERLY!
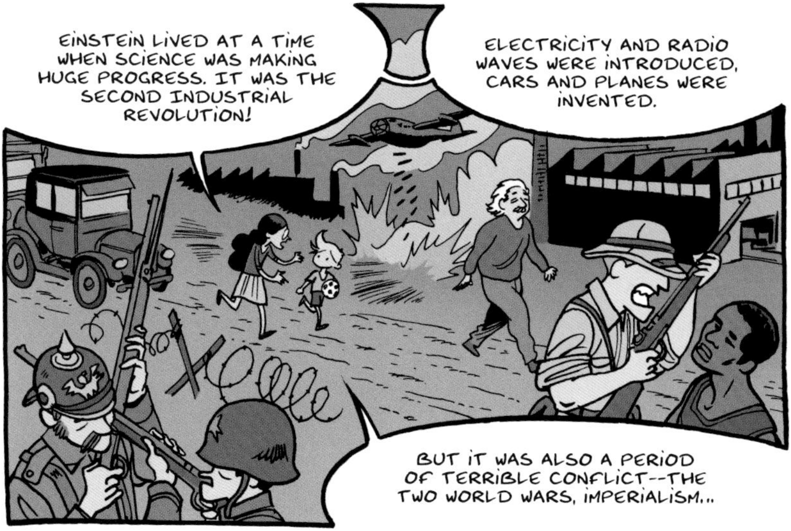
EINSTEIN LIVED AT A TIME WHEN SCIENCE WAS MAKING HUGE PROGRESS. IT WAS THE SECOND INDUSTRIAL REVOLUTION!
ELECTRICITY AND RADIO WAVES WERE INTRODUCED, CARS AND PLANES WERE INVENTED.
BUT IT WAS ALSO A PERIOD OF TERRIBLE CONFLICT--THE TWO WORLD WARS, IMPERIALISM...

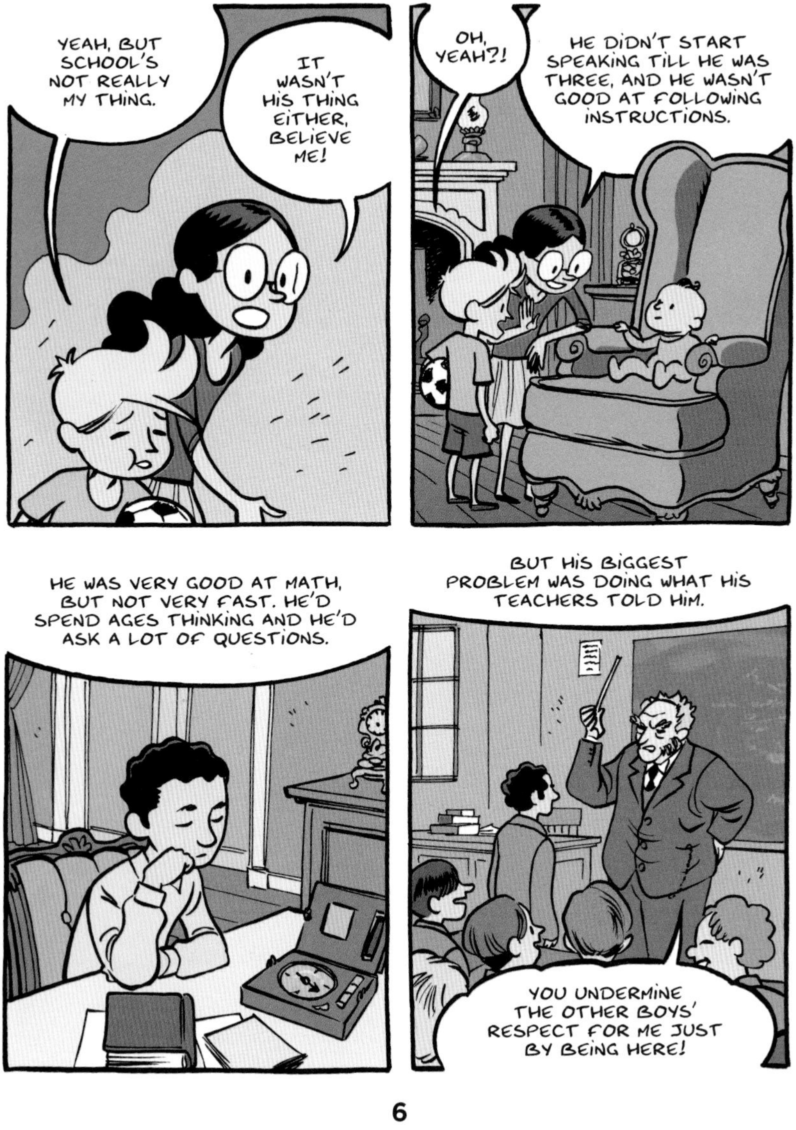
YEAH, BUT SCHOOL'S NOT REALLY MY THING.
IT WASN'T HIS THING EITHER, BELIEVE ME!
OH, YEAH?!
HE DIDN'T START SPEAKING TILL HE WAS THREE, AND HE WASN'T GOOD AT FOLLOWING INSTRUCTIONS.
HE WAS VERY GOOD AT MATH, BUT NOT VERY FAST. HE'D SPEND AGES THINKING AND HE'D ASK A LOT OF QUESTIONS.
BUT HIS BIGGEST PROBLEM WAS DOING WHAT HIS TEACHERS TOLD HIM.
YOU UNDERMINE THE OTHER BOYS' RESPECT FOR ME JUST BY BEING HERE!

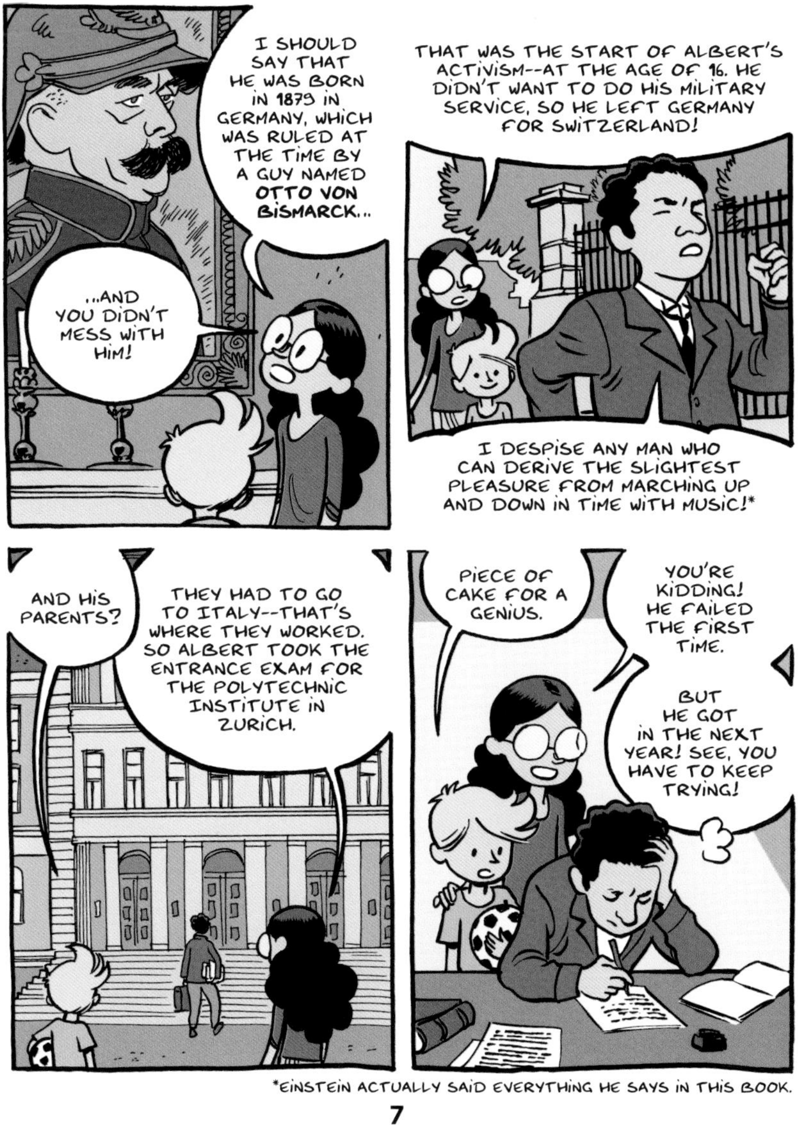
I SHOULD SAY THAT HE WAS BORN IN 1879 IN GERMANY, WHICH WAS RULED AT THE TIME BY A GUY NAMED **OTTO VON BISMARCK**...
...AND YOU DIDN'T MESS WITH HIM!
THAT WAS THE START OF ALBERT'S ACTIVISM--AT THE AGE OF 16. HE DIDN'T WANT TO DO HIS MILITARY SERVICE, SO HE LEFT GERMANY FOR SWITZERLAND!
I DESPISE ANY MAN WHO CAN DERIVE THE SLIGHTEST PLEASURE FROM MARCHING UP AND DOWN IN TIME WITH MUSIC!*
AND HIS PARENTS?
THEY HAD TO GO TO ITALY--THAT'S WHERE THEY WORKED. SO ALBERT TOOK THE ENTRANCE EXAM FOR THE POLYTECHNIC INSTITUTE IN ZURICH.
PIECE OF CAKE FOR A GENIUS.
YOU'RE KIDDING! HE FAILED THE FIRST TIME.
BUT HE GOT IN THE NEXT YEAR! SEE, YOU HAVE TO KEEP TRYING!

*EINSTEIN ACTUALLY SAID EVERYTHING HE SAYS IN THIS BOOK.

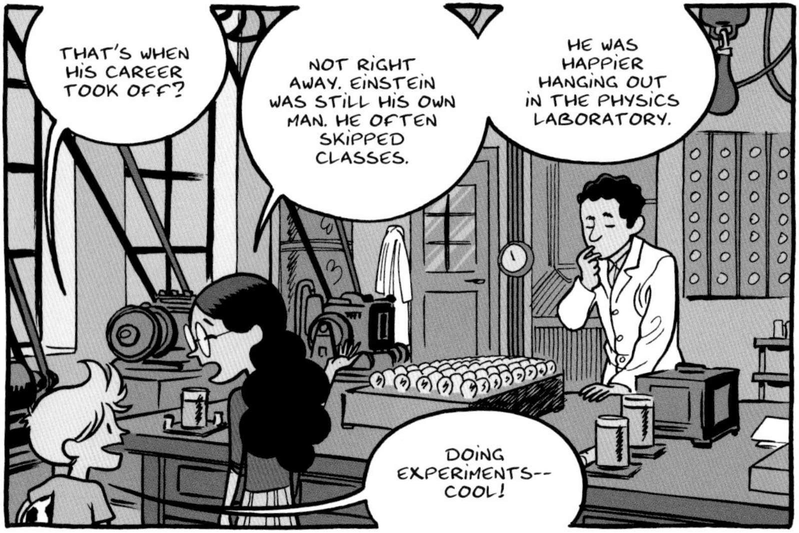
THAT'S WHEN HIS CAREER TOOK OFF?
NOT RIGHT AWAY. EINSTEIN WAS STILL HIS OWN MAN. HE OFTEN SKIPPED CLASSES.
HE WAS HAPPIER HANGING OUT IN THE PHYSICS LABORATORY.
DOING EXPERIMENTS--COOL!

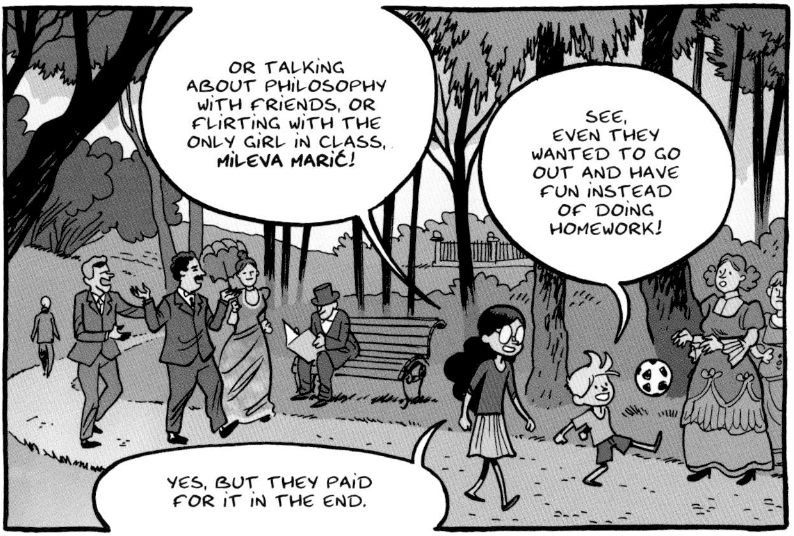
OR TALKING ABOUT PHILOSOPHY WITH FRIENDS, OR FLIRTING WITH THE ONLY GIRL IN CLASS, **MILEVA MARIĆ**!
SEE, EVEN THEY WANTED TO GO OUT AND HAVE FUN INSTEAD OF DOING HOMEWORK!
YES, BUT THEY PAID FOR IT IN THE END.

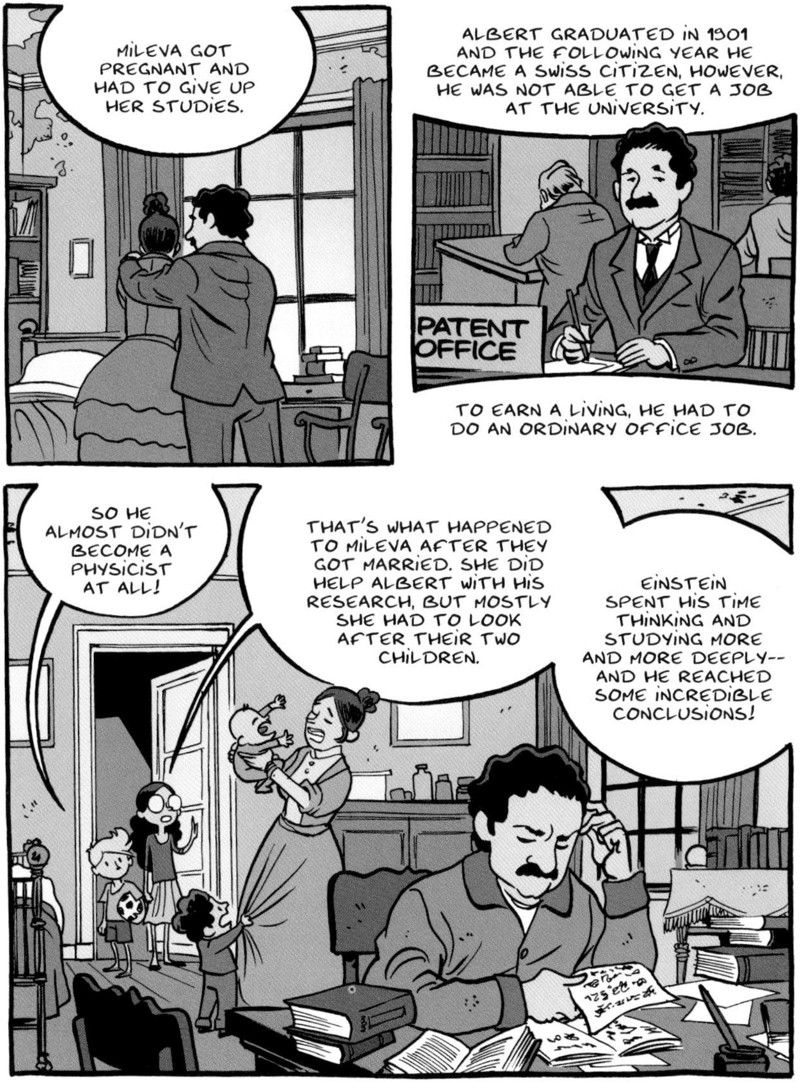
MILEVA GOT PREGNANT AND HAD TO GIVE UP HER STUDIES.
ALBERT GRADUATED IN 1901 AND THE FOLLOWING YEAR HE BECAME A SWISS CITIZEN, HOWEVER, HE WAS NOT ABLE TO GET A JOB AT THE UNIVERSITY.
PATENT OFFICE
TO EARN A LIVING, HE HAD TO DO AN ORDINARY OFFICE JOB.
SO HE ALMOST DIDN'T BECOME A PHYSICIST AT ALL!
THAT'S WHAT HAPPENED TO MILEVA AFTER THEY GOT MARRIED. SHE DID HELP ALBERT WITH HIS RESEARCH, BUT MOSTLY SHE HAD TO LOOK AFTER THEIR TWO CHILDREN.
EINSTEIN SPENT HIS TIME THINKING AND STUDYING MORE AND MORE DEEPLY--AND HE REACHED SOME INCREDIBLE CONCLUSIONS!

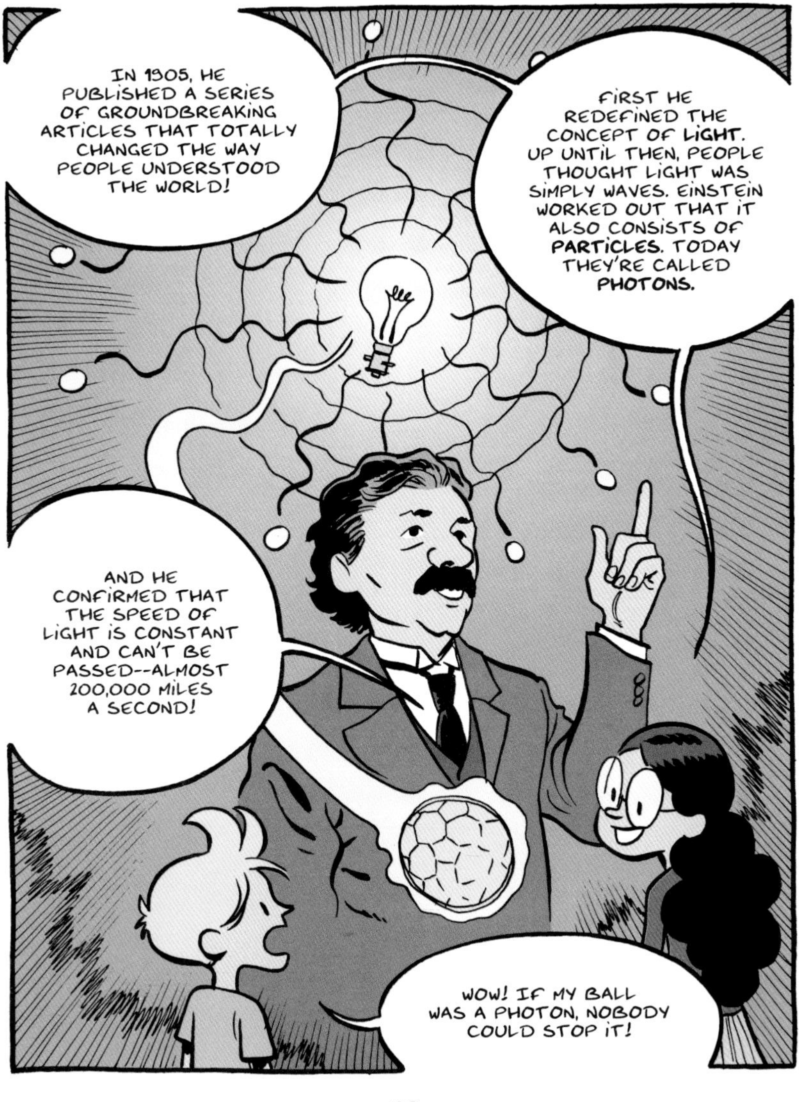
IN 1905, HE PUBLISHED A SERIES OF GROUNDBREAKING ARTICLES THAT TOTALLY CHANGED THE WAY PEOPLE UNDERSTOOD THE WORLD!
FIRST HE REDEFINED THE CONCEPT OF **LIGHT**. UP UNTIL THEN, PEOPLE THOUGHT LIGHT WAS SIMPLY WAVES. EINSTEIN WORKED OUT THAT IT ALSO CONSISTS OF **PARTICLES**. TODAY THEY'RE CALLED **PHOTONS**.
AND HE CONFIRMED THAT THE SPEED OF LIGHT IS CONSTANT AND CAN'T BE PASSED--ALMOST 200,000 MILES A SECOND!
WOW! IF MY BALL WAS A PHOTON, NOBODY COULD STOP IT!

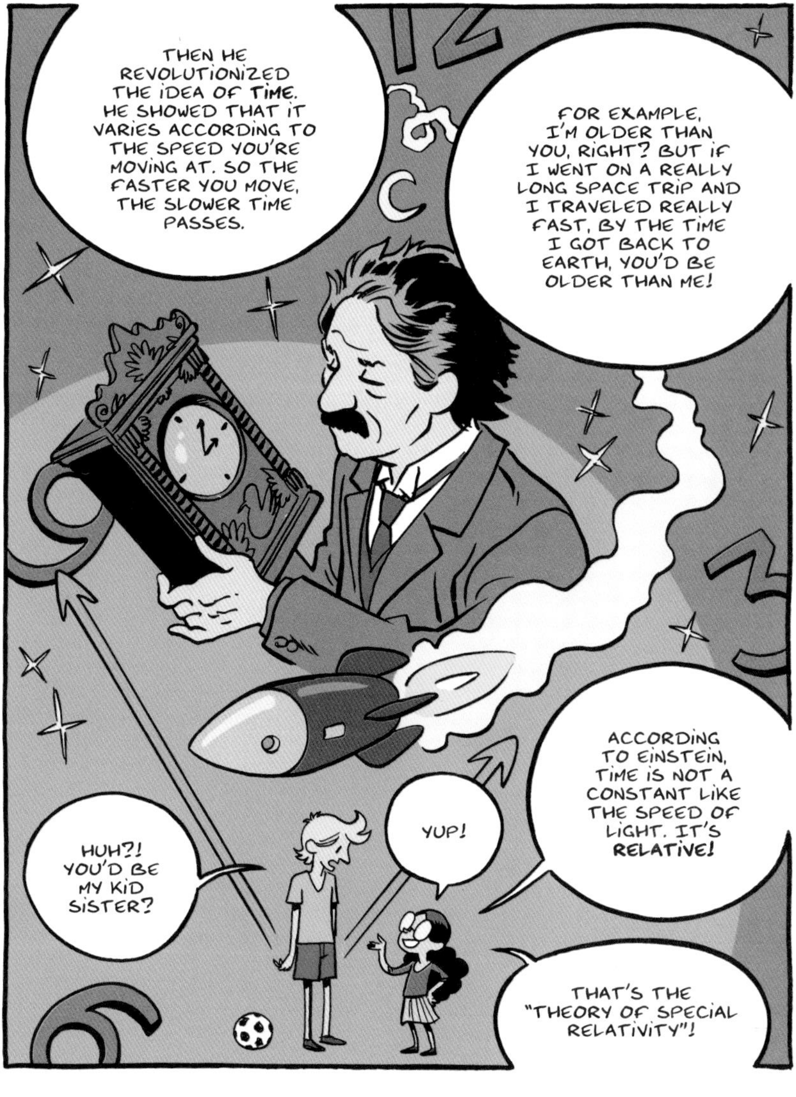
THEN HE REVOLUTIONIZED THE IDEA OF **TIME**. HE SHOWED THAT IT VARIES ACCORDING TO THE SPEED YOU'RE MOVING AT. SO THE FASTER YOU MOVE, THE SLOWER TIME PASSES.
FOR EXAMPLE, I'M OLDER THAN YOU, RIGHT? BUT IF I WENT ON A REALLY LONG SPACE TRIP AND I TRAVELED REALLY FAST, BY THE TIME I GOT BACK TO EARTH, YOU'D BE OLDER THAN ME!
ACCORDING TO EINSTEIN, TIME IS NOT A CONSTANT LIKE THE SPEED OF LIGHT. IT'S **RELATIVE!**
HUH?! YOU'D BE MY KID SISTER?
YUP!
THAT'S THE "THEORY OF SPECIAL RELATIVITY"!

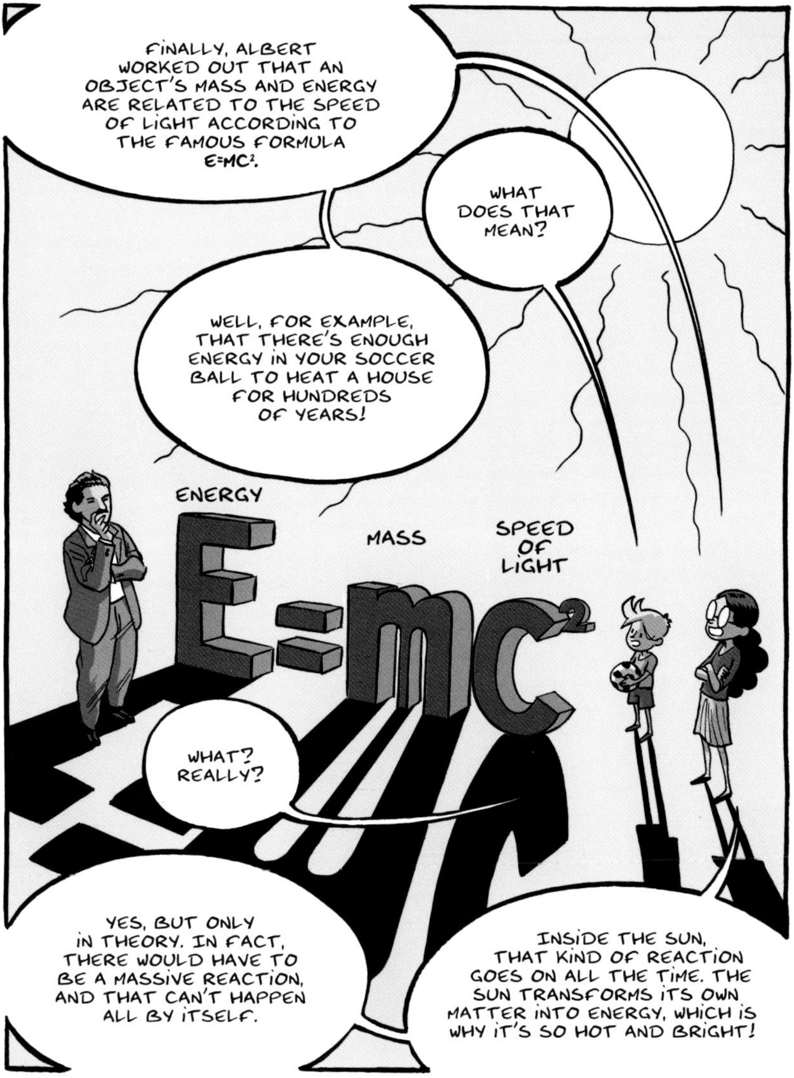
FINALLY, ALBERT WORKED OUT THAT AN OBJECT'S MASS AND ENERGY ARE RELATED TO THE SPEED OF LIGHT ACCORDING TO THE FAMOUS FORMULA E=MC².
WHAT DOES THAT MEAN?
WELL, FOR EXAMPLE, THAT THERE'S ENOUGH ENERGY IN YOUR SOCCER BALL TO HEAT A HOUSE FOR HUNDREDS OF YEARS!
ENERGY
MASS
SPEED OF LIGHT
E=mc²
WHAT? REALLY?
YES, BUT ONLY IN THEORY. IN FACT, THERE WOULD HAVE TO BE A MASSIVE REACTION, AND THAT CAN'T HAPPEN ALL BY ITSELF.
INSIDE THE SUN, THAT KIND OF REACTION GOES ON ALL THE TIME. THE SUN TRANSFORMS ITS OWN MATTER INTO ENERGY, WHICH IS WHY IT'S SO HOT AND BRIGHT!

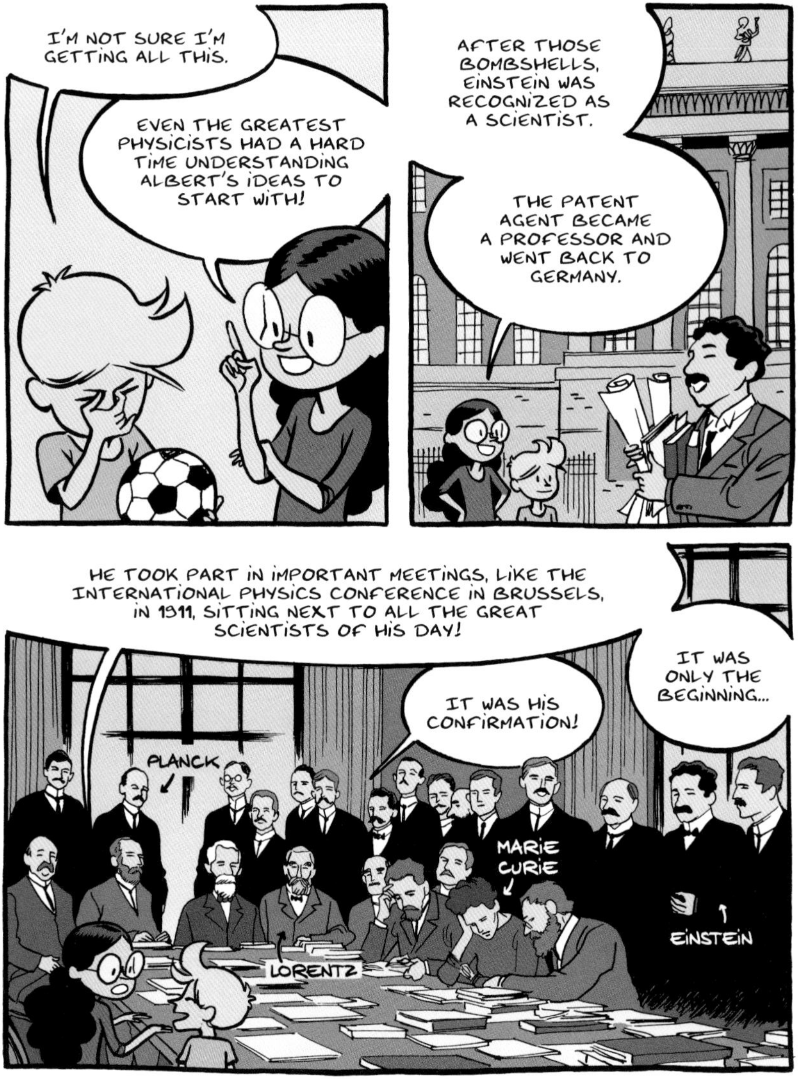
I'M NOT SURE I'M GETTING ALL THIS.
EVEN THE GREATEST PHYSICISTS HAD A HARD TIME UNDERSTANDING ALBERT'S IDEAS TO START WITH!
AFTER THOSE BOMBSHELLS, EINSTEIN WAS RECOGNIZED AS A SCIENTIST.
THE PATENT AGENT BECAME A PROFESSOR AND WENT BACK TO GERMANY.
HE TOOK PART IN IMPORTANT MEETINGS, LIKE THE INTERNATIONAL PHYSICS CONFERENCE IN BRUSSELS, IN 1911, SITTING NEXT TO ALL THE GREAT SCIENTISTS OF HIS DAY!
IT WAS ONLY THE BEGINNING...
IT WAS HIS CONFIRMATION!
PLANCK
MARIE CURIE
EINSTEIN
LORENTZ

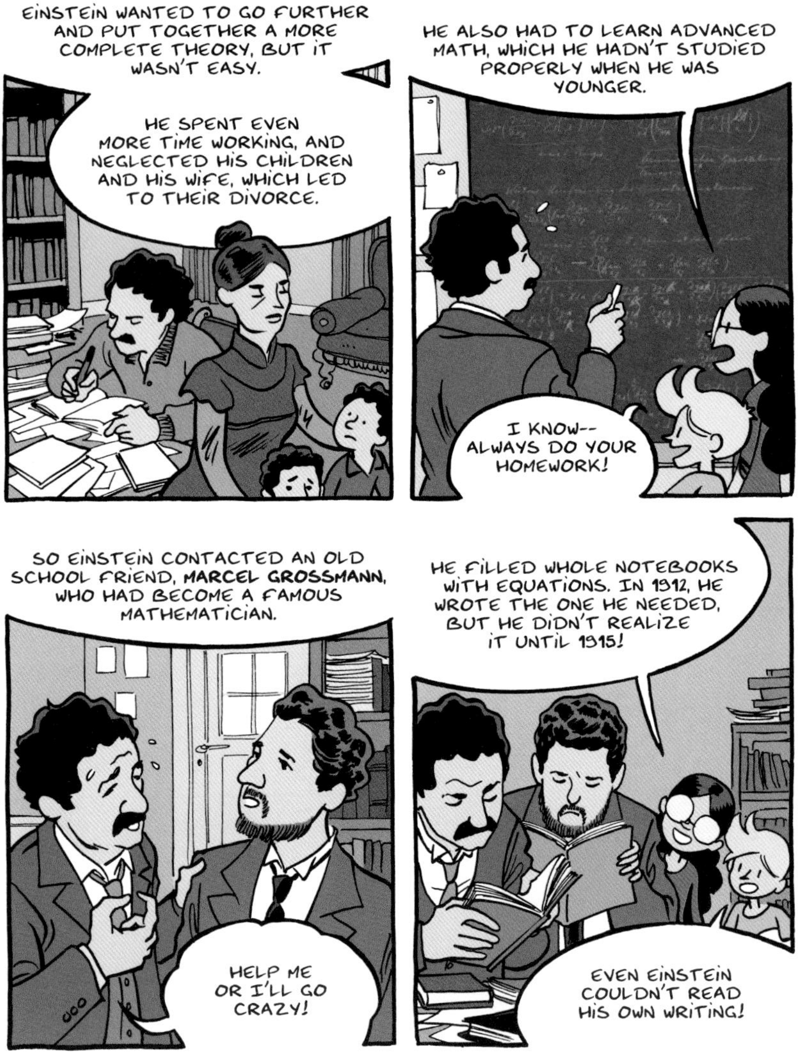
EINSTEIN WANTED TO GO FURTHER AND PUT TOGETHER A MORE COMPLETE THEORY, BUT IT WASN'T EASY.
HE SPENT EVEN MORE TIME WORKING, AND NEGLECTED HIS CHILDREN AND HIS WIFE, WHICH LED TO THEIR DIVORCE.
HE ALSO HAD TO LEARN ADVANCED MATH, WHICH HE HADN'T STUDIED PROPERLY WHEN HE WAS YOUNGER.
I KNOW-- ALWAYS DO YOUR HOMEWORK!
SO EINSTEIN CONTACTED AN OLD SCHOOL FRIEND, MARCEL GROSSMANN, WHO HAD BECOME A FAMOUS MATHEMATICIAN.
HELP ME OR I'LL GO CRAZY!
HE FILLED WHOLE NOTEBOOKS WITH EQUATIONS. IN 1912, HE WROTE THE ONE HE NEEDED, BUT HE DIDN'T REALIZE IT UNTIL 1915!
EVEN EINSTEIN COULDN'T READ HIS OWN WRITING!

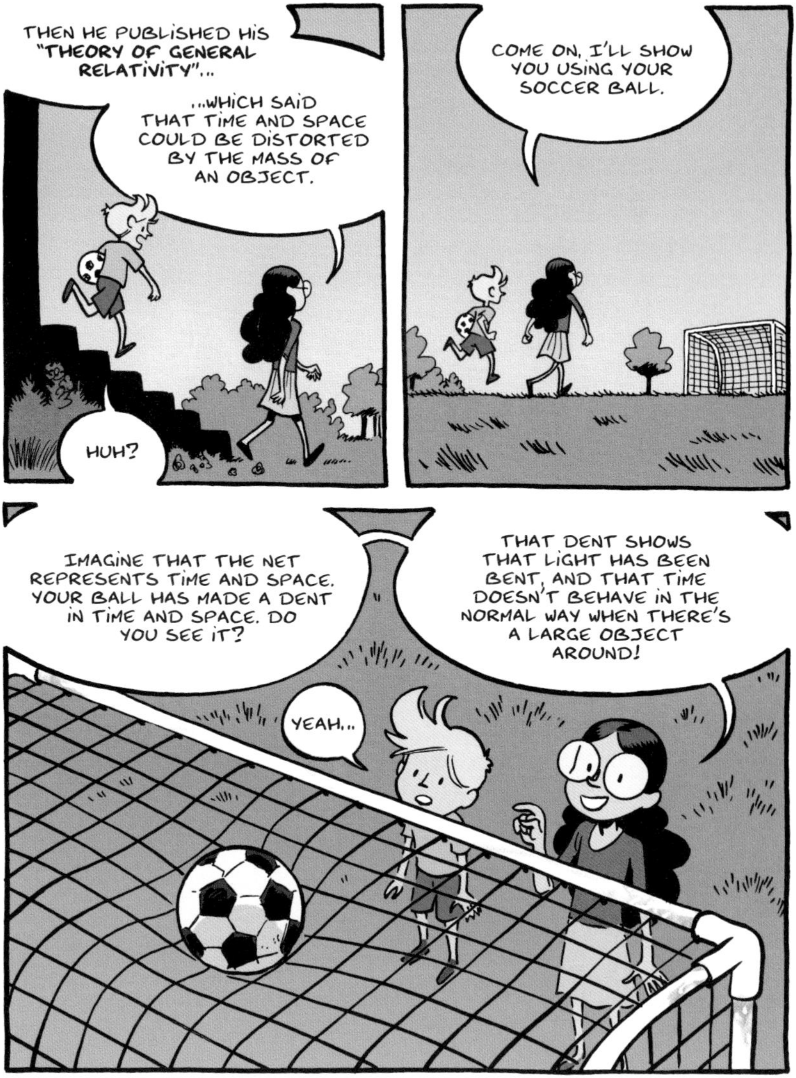
THEN HE PUBLISHED HIS "THEORY OF GENERAL RELATIVITY"...
...WHICH SAID THAT TIME AND SPACE COULD BE DISTORTED BY THE MASS OF AN OBJECT.
HUH?
COME ON, I'LL SHOW YOU USING YOUR SOCCER BALL.
IMAGINE THAT THE NET REPRESENTS TIME AND SPACE. YOUR BALL HAS MADE A DENT IN TIME AND SPACE. DO YOU SEE IT?
YEAH...
THAT DENT SHOWS THAT LIGHT HAS BEEN BENT, AND THAT TIME DOESN'T BEHAVE IN THE NORMAL WAY WHEN THERE'S A LARGE OBJECT AROUND!

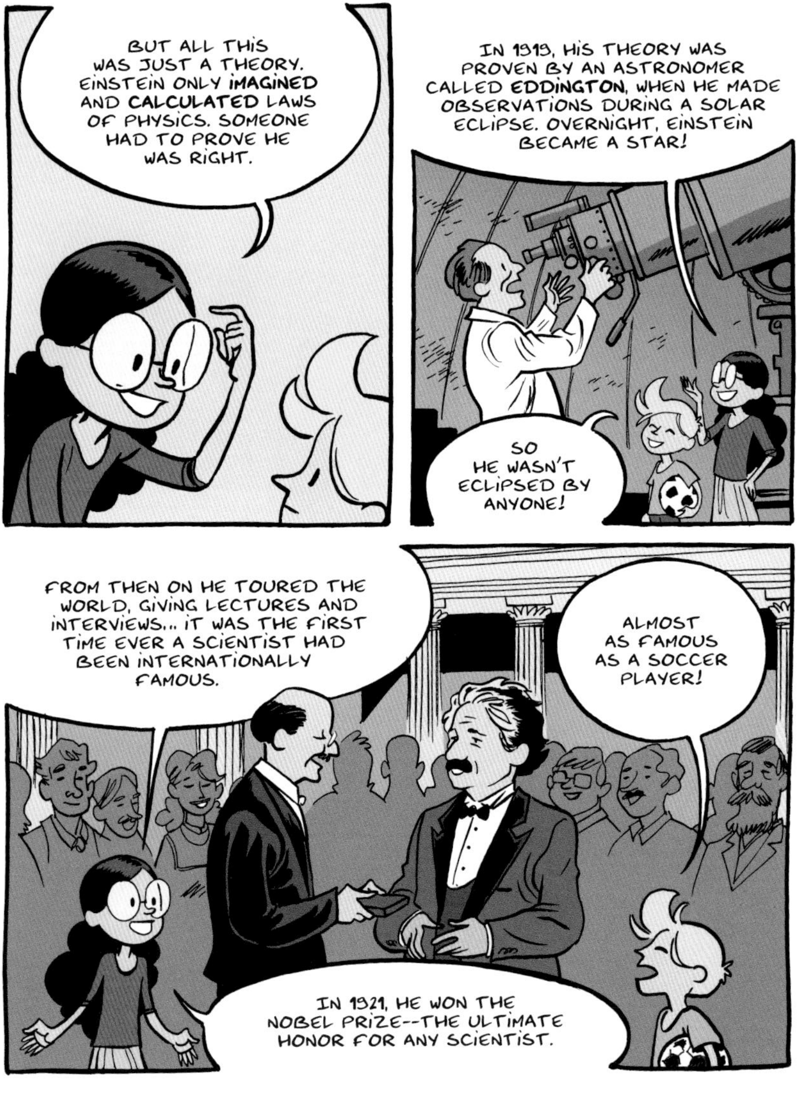
BUT ALL THIS WAS JUST A THEORY. EINSTEIN ONLY **IMAGINED** AND **CALCULATED** LAWS OF PHYSICS. SOMEONE HAD TO PROVE HE WAS RIGHT.
IN 1919, HIS THEORY WAS PROVEN BY AN ASTRONOMER CALLED **EDDINGTON**, WHEN HE MADE OBSERVATIONS DURING A SOLAR ECLIPSE. OVERNIGHT, EINSTEIN BECAME A STAR!
SO HE WASN'T ECLIPSED BY ANYONE!
FROM THEN ON HE TOURED THE WORLD, GIVING LECTURES AND INTERVIEWS... IT WAS THE FIRST TIME EVER A SCIENTIST HAD BEEN INTERNATIONALLY FAMOUS.
ALMOST AS FAMOUS AS A SOCCER PLAYER!
IN 1921, HE WON THE NOBEL PRIZE--THE ULTIMATE HONOR FOR ANY SCIENTIST.

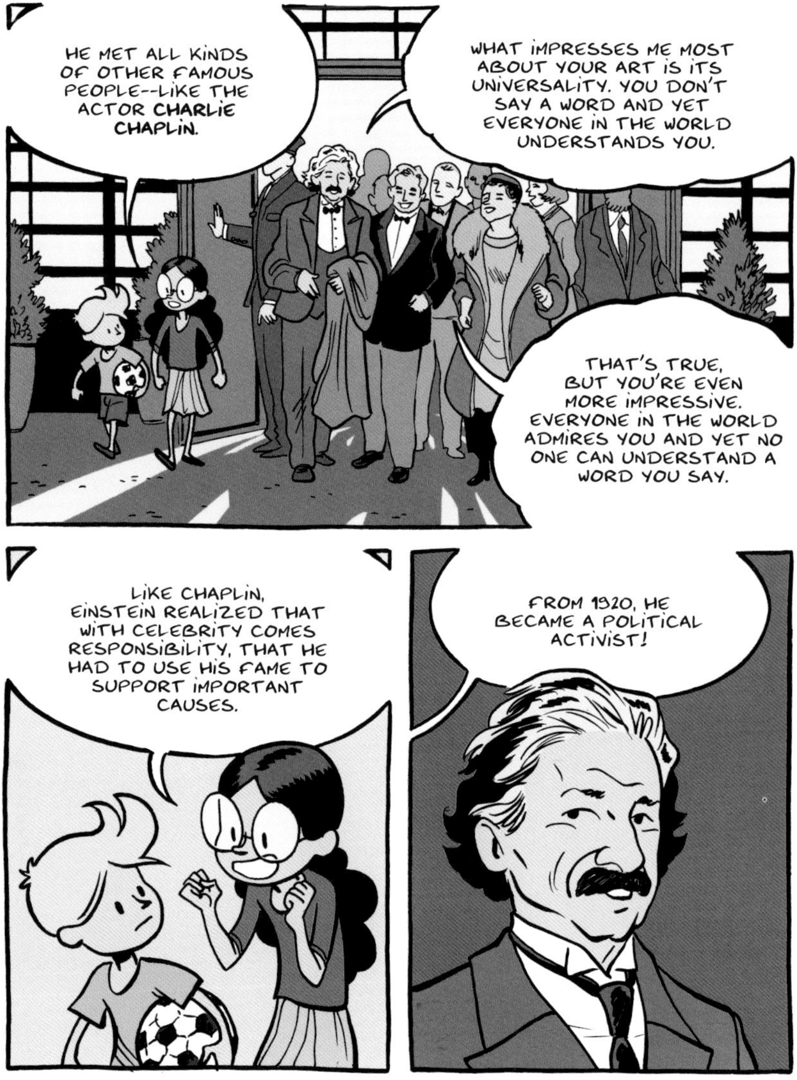
HE MET ALL KINDS OF OTHER FAMOUS PEOPLE--LIKE THE ACTOR CHARLIE CHAPLIN.
WHAT IMPRESSES ME MOST ABOUT YOUR ART IS ITS UNIVERSALITY. YOU DON'T SAY A WORD AND YET EVERYONE IN THE WORLD UNDERSTANDS YOU.
THAT'S TRUE, BUT YOU'RE EVEN MORE IMPRESSIVE. EVERYONE IN THE WORLD ADMIRES YOU AND YET NO ONE CAN UNDERSTAND A WORD YOU SAY.
LIKE CHAPLIN, EINSTEIN REALIZED THAT WITH CELEBRITY COMES RESPONSIBILITY, THAT HE HAD TO USE HIS FAME TO SUPPORT IMPORTANT CAUSES.
FROM 1920, HE BECAME A POLITICAL ACTIVIST!

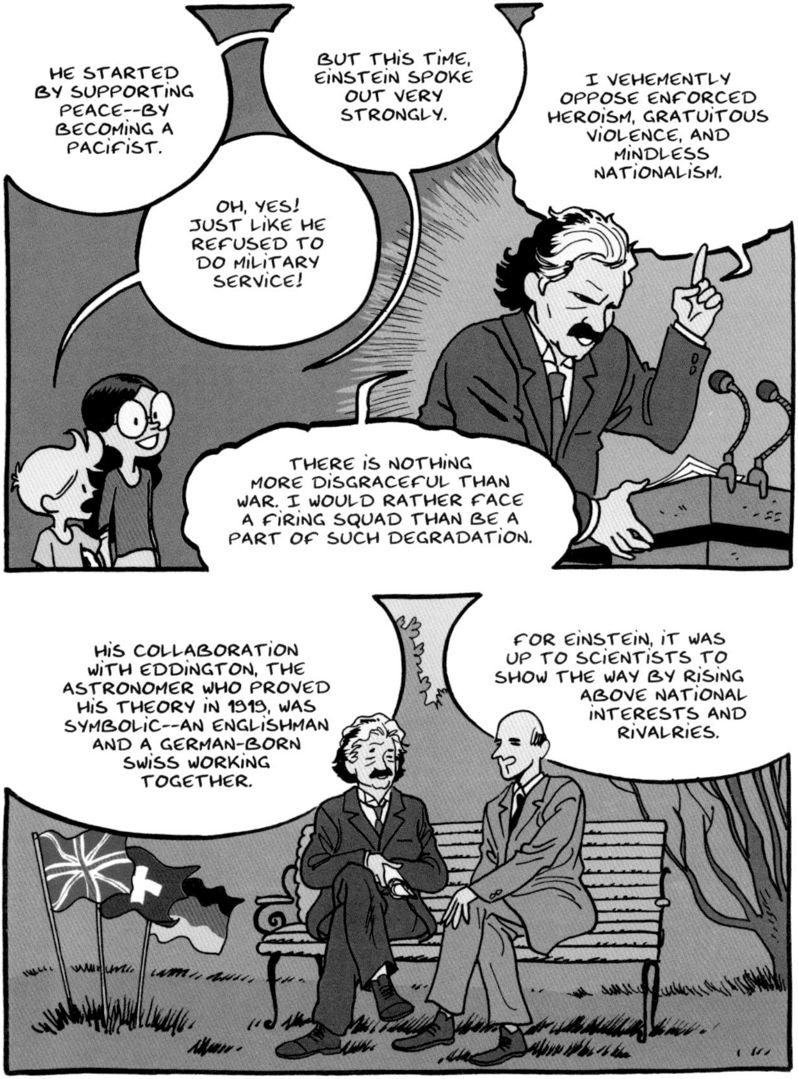
HE STARTED BY SUPPORTING PEACE--BY BECOMING A PACIFIST.
BUT THIS TIME, EINSTEIN SPOKE OUT VERY STRONGLY.
OH, YES! JUST LIKE HE REFUSED TO DO MILITARY SERVICE!
I VEHEMENTLY OPPOSE ENFORCED HEROISM, GRATUITOUS VIOLENCE, AND MINDLESS NATIONALISM.
THERE IS NOTHING MORE DISGRACEFUL THAN WAR. I WOULD RATHER FACE A FIRING SQUAD THAN BE A PART OF SUCH DEGRADATION.
HIS COLLABORATION WITH EDDINGTON, THE ASTRONOMER WHO PROVED HIS THEORY IN 1919, WAS SYMBOLIC--AN ENGLISHMAN AND A GERMAN-BORN SWISS WORKING TOGETHER.
FOR EINSTEIN, IT WAS UP TO SCIENTISTS TO SHOW THE WAY BY RISING ABOVE NATIONAL INTERESTS AND RIVALRIES.

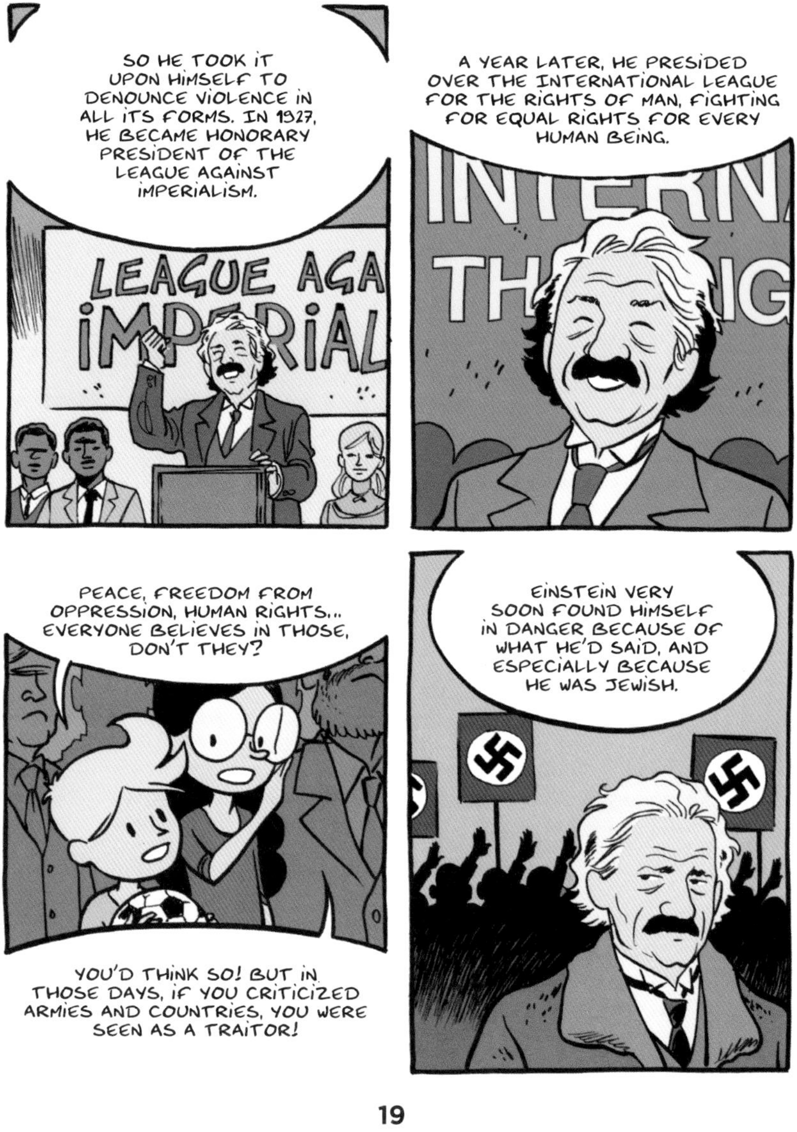
SO HE TOOK IT UPON HIMSELF TO DENOUNCE VIOLENCE IN ALL ITS FORMS. IN 1927, HE BECAME HONORARY PRESIDENT OF THE LEAGUE AGAINST IMPERIALISM.
LEAGUE AGA
IMPERIAL
A YEAR LATER, HE PRESIDED OVER THE INTERNATIONAL LEAGUE FOR THE RIGHTS OF MAN, FIGHTING FOR EQUAL RIGHTS FOR EVERY HUMAN BEING.
INTERN
TH IG
PEACE, FREEDOM FROM OPPRESSION, HUMAN RIGHTS... EVERYONE BELIEVES IN THOSE, DON'T THEY?
YOU'D THINK SO! BUT IN THOSE DAYS, IF YOU CRITICIZED ARMIES AND COUNTRIES, YOU WERE SEEN AS A TRAITOR!
EINSTEIN VERY SOON FOUND HIMSELF IN DANGER BECAUSE OF WHAT HE'D SAID, AND ESPECIALLY BECAUSE HE WAS JEWISH.

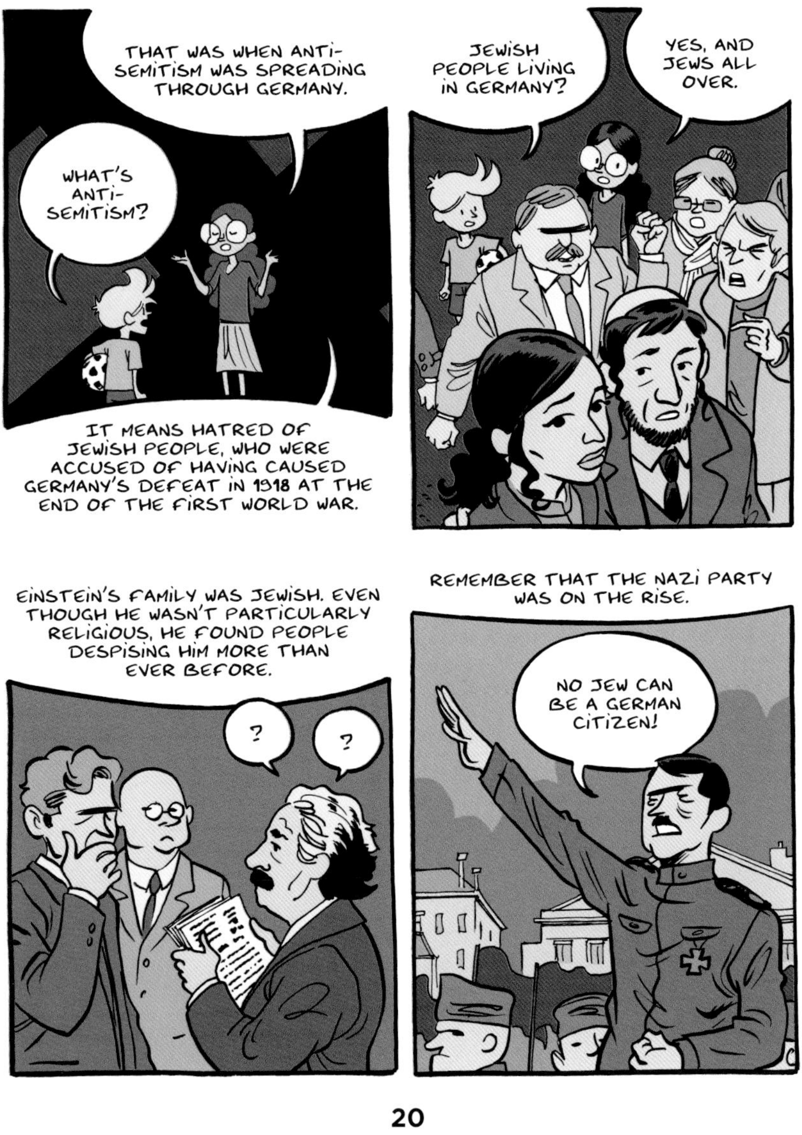

THAT WAS WHEN ANTI-SEMITISM WAS SPREADING THROUGH GERMANY.
WHAT'S ANTI-SEMITISM?
IT MEANS HATRED OF JEWISH PEOPLE, WHO WERE ACCUSED OF HAVING CAUSED GERMANY'S DEFEAT IN 1918 AT THE END OF THE FIRST WORLD WAR.
JEWISH PEOPLE LIVING IN GERMANY?
YES, AND JEWS ALL OVER.
EINSTEIN'S FAMILY WAS JEWISH. EVEN THOUGH HE WASN'T PARTICULARLY RELIGIOUS, HE FOUND PEOPLE DESPISING HIM MORE THAN EVER BEFORE.
?
?
REMEMBER THAT THE NAZI PARTY WAS ON THE RISE.
NO JEW CAN BE A GERMAN CITIZEN!

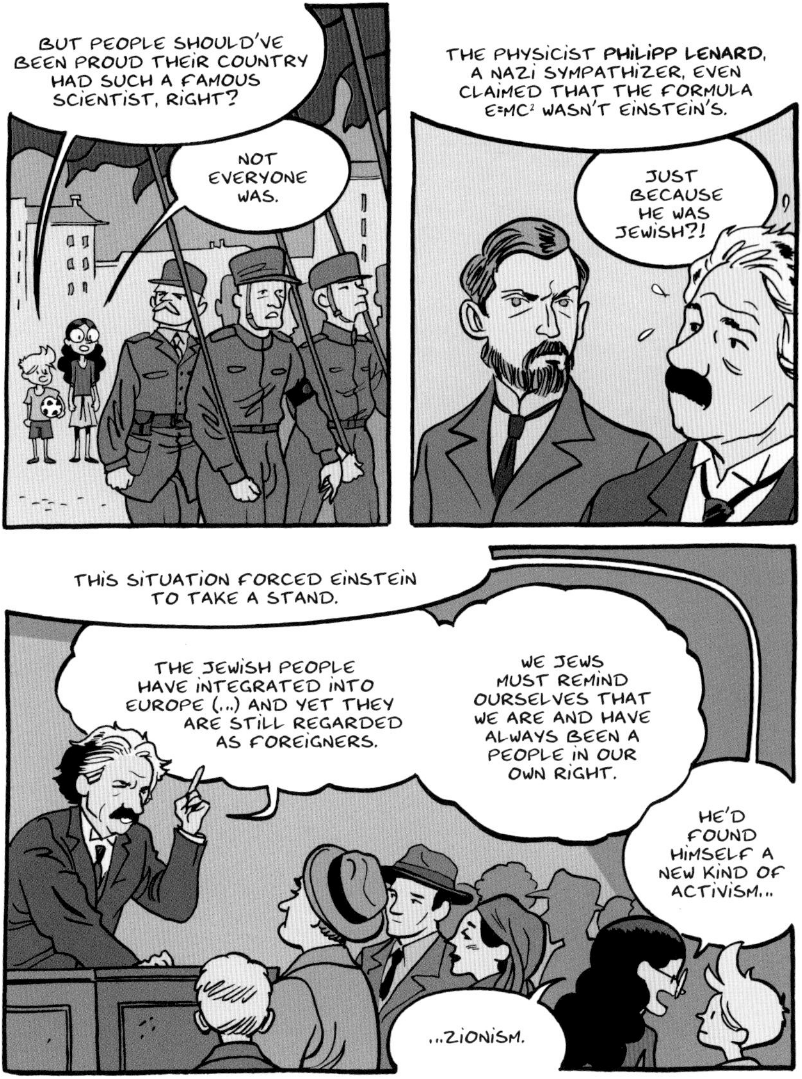
BUT PEOPLE SHOULD'VE BEEN PROUD THEIR COUNTRY HAD SUCH A FAMOUS SCIENTIST, RIGHT?
NOT EVERYONE WAS.
THE PHYSICIST **PHILIPP LENARD**, A NAZI SYMPATHIZER, EVEN CLAIMED THAT THE FORMULA $E=MC^2$ WASN'T EINSTEIN'S.
JUST BECAUSE HE WAS JEWISH?!
THIS SITUATION FORCED EINSTEIN TO TAKE A STAND.
THE JEWISH PEOPLE HAVE INTEGRATED INTO EUROPE (...) AND YET THEY ARE STILL REGARDED AS FOREIGNERS.
WE JEWS MUST REMIND OURSELVES THAT WE ARE AND HAVE ALWAYS BEEN A PEOPLE IN OUR OWN RIGHT.
HE'D FOUND HIMSELF A NEW KIND OF ACTIVISM...
...ZIONISM.

IS THAT ANOTHER SCIENTIFIC THEORY?

NO, NO, IT WAS A POLITICAL MOVEMENT THAT WANTED JEWISH PEOPLE TO HAVE THEIR OWN COUNTRY...

...FOR THE FIRST TIME.

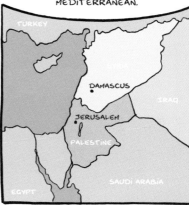

IN FACT, THE BRITISH HAD PROMISED BACK IN 1917 TO HELP CREATE ONE FOR THEM IN PALESTINE, IN THE EASTERN MEDITERRANEAN.

TURKEY

DAMASCUS

IRAQ

JERUSALEM

PALESTINE

SAUDI ARABIA

EGYPT

SO EINSTEIN SUPPORTED THE FOUNDATION OF A UNIVERSITY IN JERUSALEM AS PART OF THE FIRST STEPS TO CREATING A COUNTRY.

OF JERUSALEM

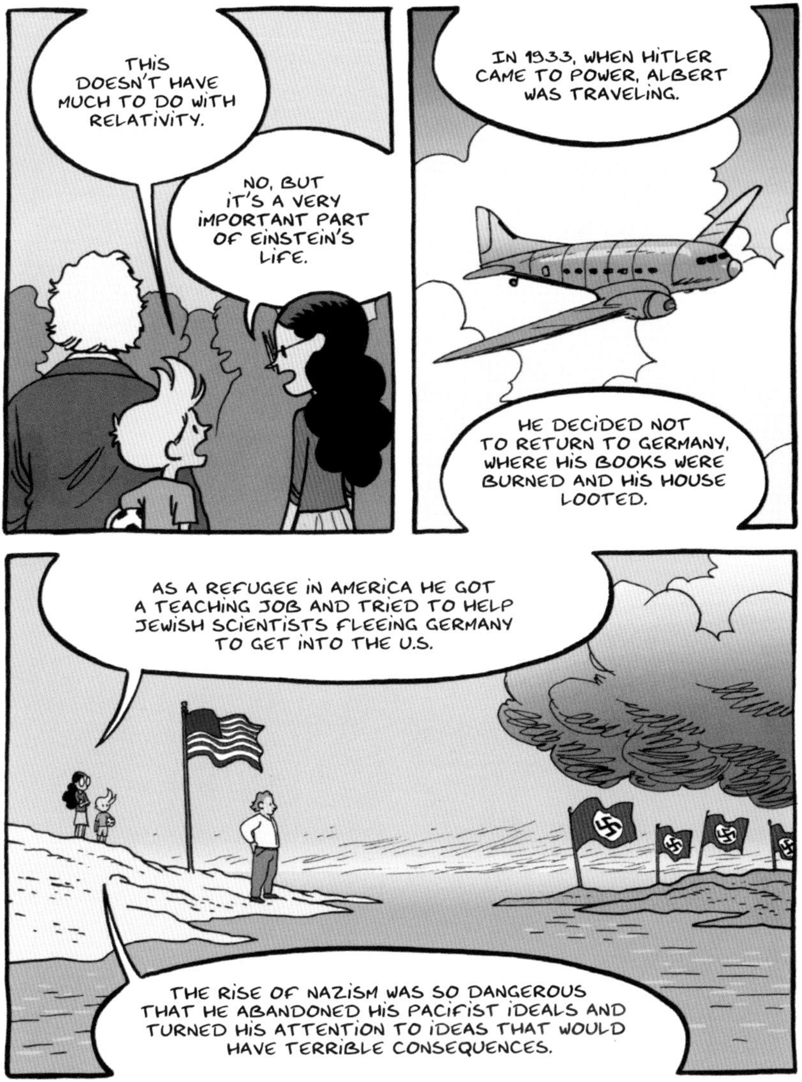
THIS DOESN'T HAVE MUCH TO DO WITH RELATIVITY.
NO, BUT IT'S A VERY IMPORTANT PART OF EINSTEIN'S LIFE.
IN 1933, WHEN HITLER CAME TO POWER, ALBERT WAS TRAVELING.
HE DECIDED NOT TO RETURN TO GERMANY, WHERE HIS BOOKS WERE BURNED AND HIS HOUSE LOOTED.
AS A REFUGEE IN AMERICA HE GOT A TEACHING JOB AND TRIED TO HELP JEWISH SCIENTISTS FLEEING GERMANY TO GET INTO THE U.S.
THE RISE OF NAZISM WAS SO DANGEROUS THAT HE ABANDONED HIS PACIFIST IDEALS AND TURNED HIS ATTENTION TO IDEAS THAT WOULD HAVE TERRIBLE CONSEQUENCES.

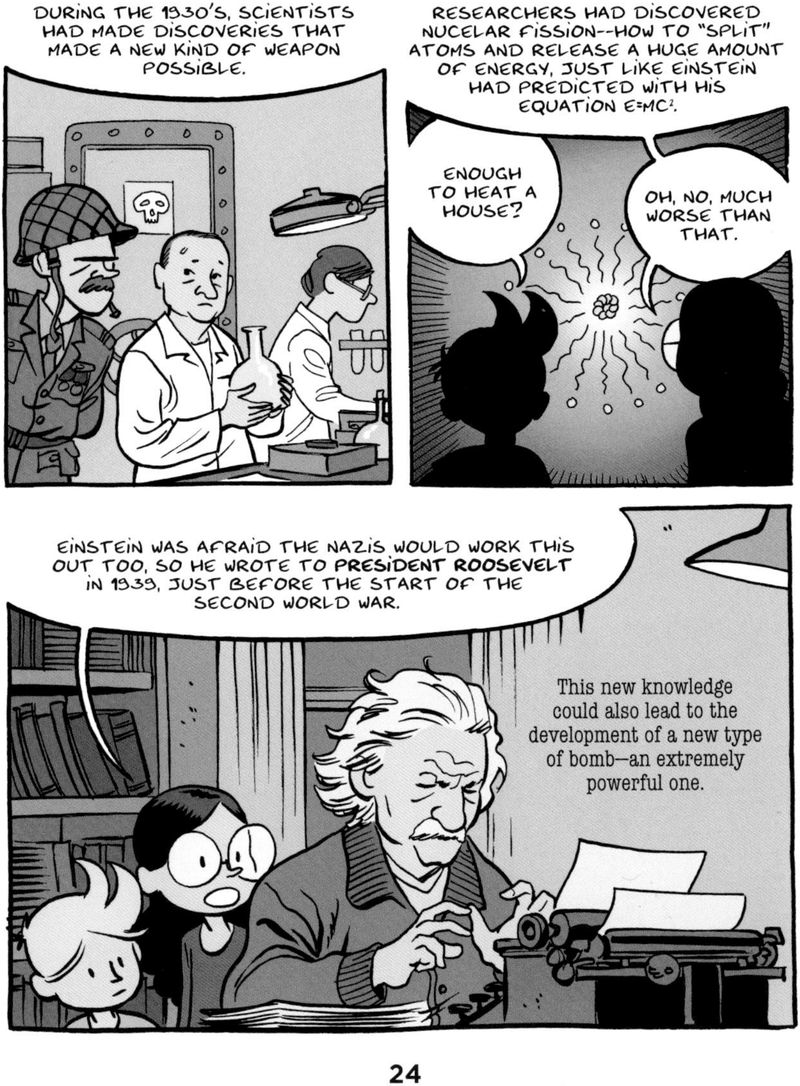
DURING THE 1930'S, SCIENTISTS HAD MADE DISCOVERIES THAT MADE A NEW KIND OF WEAPON POSSIBLE.
RESEARCHERS HAD DISCOVERED NUCELAR FISSION--HOW TO "SPLIT" ATOMS AND RELEASE A HUGE AMOUNT OF ENERGY, JUST LIKE EINSTEIN HAD PREDICTED WITH HIS EQUATION $E=MC^2$.
ENOUGH TO HEAT A HOUSE?
OH, NO, MUCH WORSE THAN THAT.
EINSTEIN WAS AFRAID THE NAZIS WOULD WORK THIS OUT TOO, SO HE WROTE TO **PRESIDENT ROOSEVELT** IN 1939, JUST BEFORE THE START OF THE SECOND WORLD WAR.
This new knowledge could also lead to the development of a new type of bomb—an extremely powerful one.

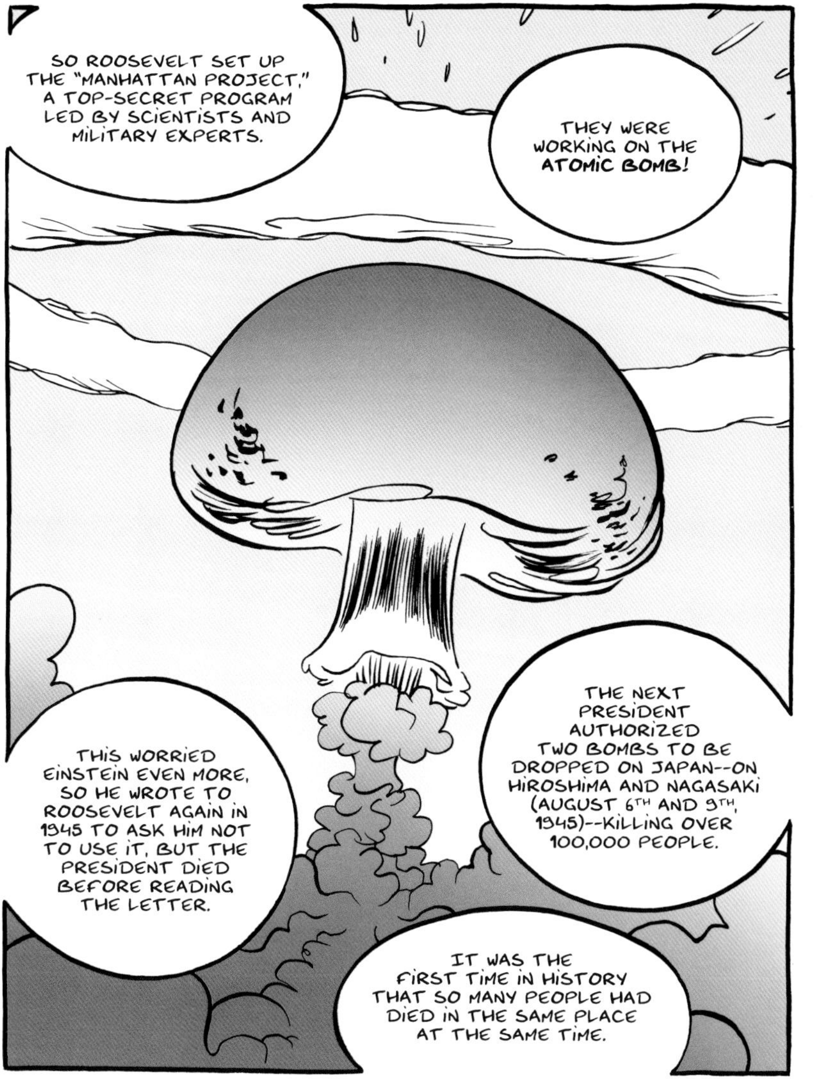
SO ROOSEVELT SET UP THE "MANHATTAN PROJECT," A TOP-SECRET PROGRAM LED BY SCIENTISTS AND MILITARY EXPERTS.
THEY WERE WORKING ON THE **ATOMIC BOMB!**
THIS WORRIED EINSTEIN EVEN MORE, SO HE WROTE TO ROOSEVELT AGAIN IN 1945 TO ASK HIM NOT TO USE IT, BUT THE PRESIDENT DIED BEFORE READING THE LETTER.
THE NEXT PRESIDENT AUTHORIZED TWO BOMBS TO BE DROPPED ON JAPAN--ON HIROSHIMA AND NAGASAKI (AUGUST 6TH AND 9TH, 1945)--KILLING OVER 100,000 PEOPLE.
IT WAS THE FIRST TIME IN HISTORY THAT SO MANY PEOPLE HAD DIED IN THE SAME PLACE AT THE SAME TIME.

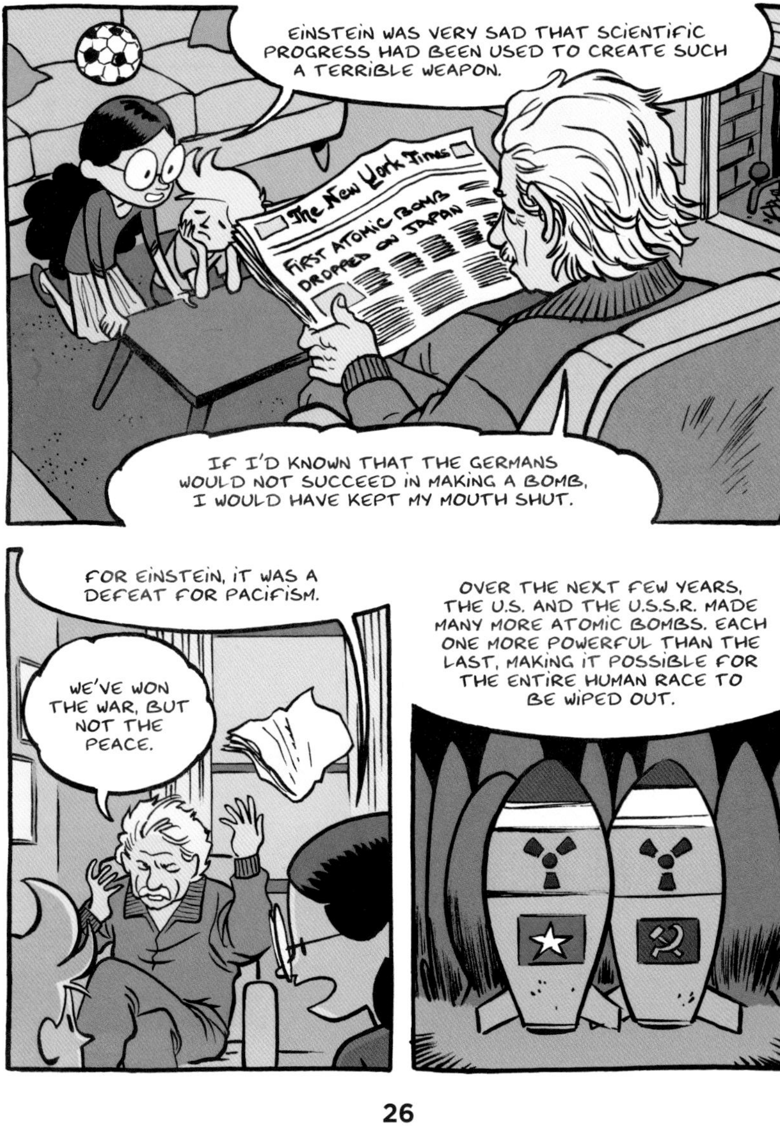
EINSTEIN WAS VERY SAD THAT SCIENTIFIC PROGRESS HAD BEEN USED TO CREATE SUCH A TERRIBLE WEAPON.
The New York Times
FIRST ATOMIC BOMB DROPPED ON JAPAN
IF I'D KNOWN THAT THE GERMANS WOULD NOT SUCCEED IN MAKING A BOMB, I WOULD HAVE KEPT MY MOUTH SHUT.
FOR EINSTEIN, IT WAS A DEFEAT FOR PACIFISM.
WE'VE WON THE WAR, BUT NOT THE PEACE.
OVER THE NEXT FEW YEARS, THE U.S. AND THE U.S.S.R. MADE MANY MORE ATOMIC BOMBS. EACH ONE MORE POWERFUL THAN THE LAST, MAKING IT POSSIBLE FOR THE ENTIRE HUMAN RACE TO BE WIPED OUT.

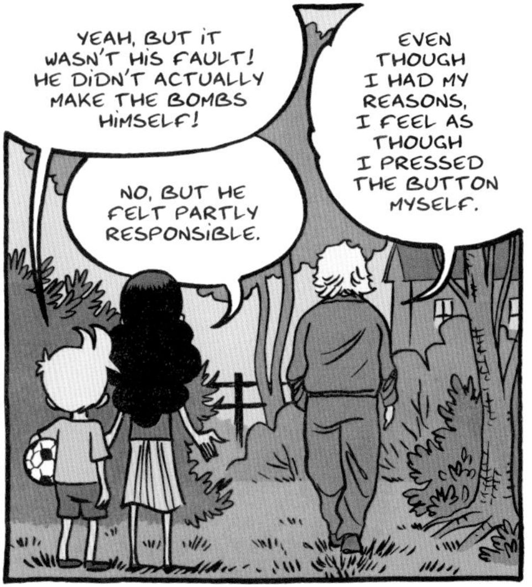
YEAH, BUT IT WASN'T HIS FAULT! HE DIDN'T ACTUALLY MAKE THE BOMBS HIMSELF!
NO, BUT HE FELT PARTLY RESPONSIBLE.
EVEN THOUGH I HAD MY REASONS, I FEEL AS THOUGH I PRESSED THE BUTTON MYSELF.

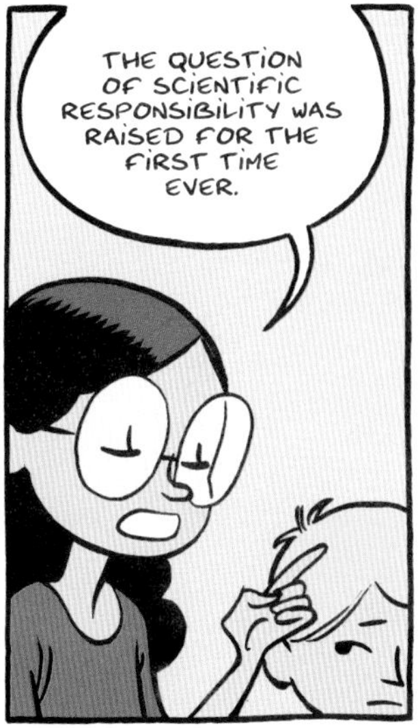
THE QUESTION OF SCIENTIFIC RESPONSIBILITY WAS RAISED FOR THE FIRST TIME EVER.

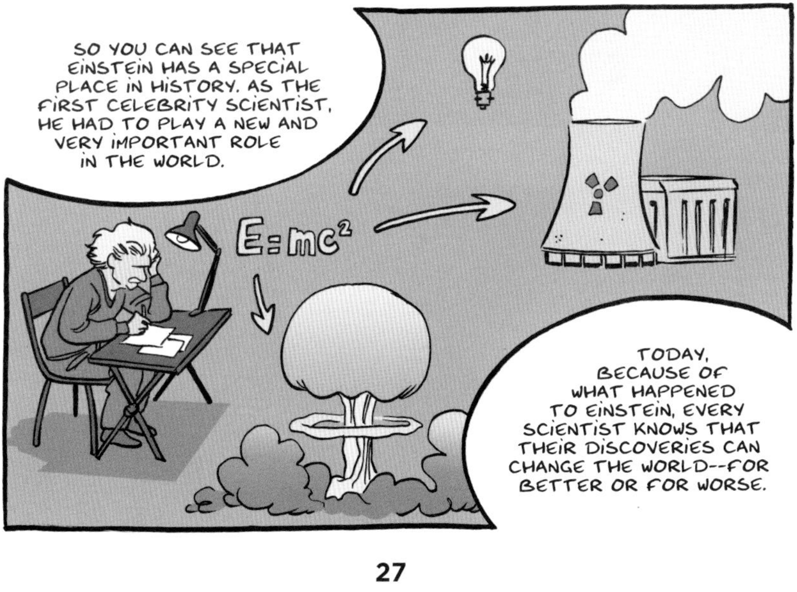
SO YOU CAN SEE THAT EINSTEIN HAS A SPECIAL PLACE IN HISTORY. AS THE FIRST CELEBRITY SCIENTIST, HE HAD TO PLAY A NEW AND VERY IMPORTANT ROLE IN THE WORLD.
E=mc²
TODAY, BECAUSE OF WHAT HAPPENED TO EINSTEIN, EVERY SCIENTIST KNOWS THAT THEIR DISCOVERIES CAN CHANGE THE WORLD--FOR BETTER OR FOR WORSE.

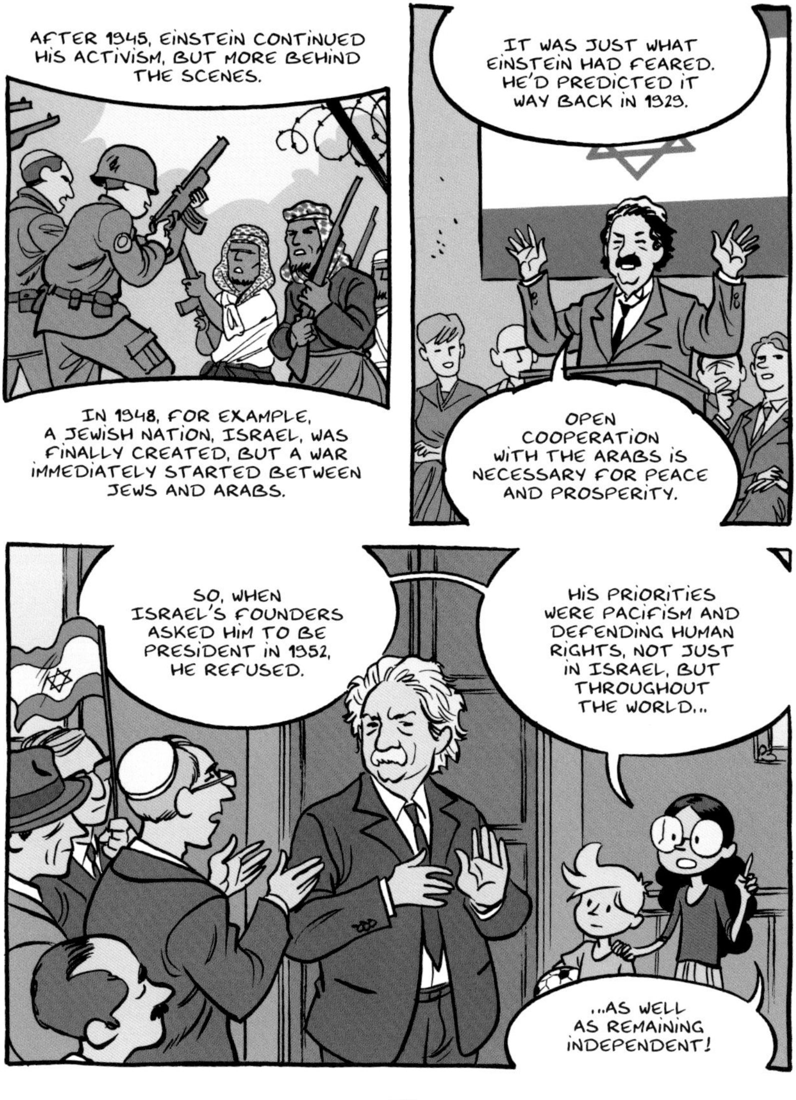
AFTER 1945, EINSTEIN CONTINUED HIS ACTIVISM, BUT MORE BEHIND THE SCENES.
IN 1948, FOR EXAMPLE, A JEWISH NATION, ISRAEL, WAS FINALLY CREATED, BUT A WAR IMMEDIATELY STARTED BETWEEN JEWS AND ARABS.
IT WAS JUST WHAT EINSTEIN HAD FEARED. HE'D PREDICTED IT WAY BACK IN 1929.
OPEN COOPERATION WITH THE ARABS IS NECESSARY FOR PEACE AND PROSPERITY.
SO, WHEN ISRAEL'S FOUNDERS ASKED HIM TO BE PRESIDENT IN 1952, HE REFUSED.
HIS PRIORITIES WERE PACIFISM AND DEFENDING HUMAN RIGHTS, NOT JUST IN ISRAEL, BUT THROUGHOUT THE WORLD...
...AS WELL AS REMAINING INDEPENDENT!

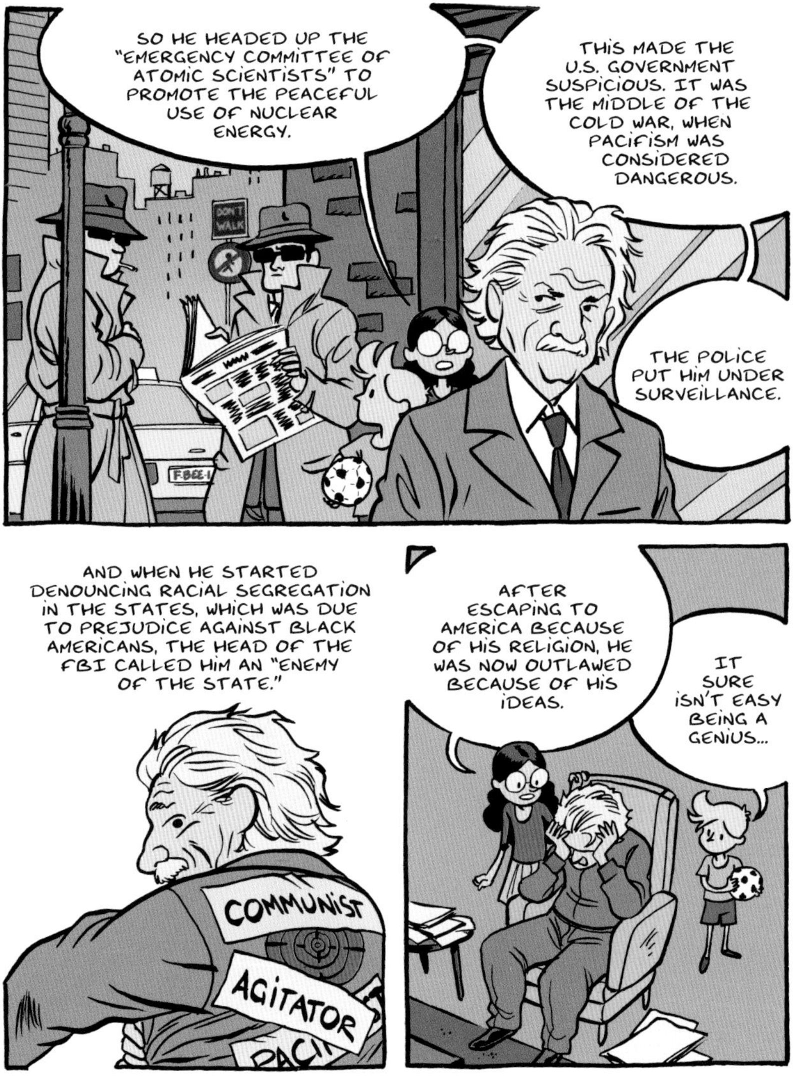
SO HE HEADED UP THE "EMERGENCY COMMITTEE OF ATOMIC SCIENTISTS" TO PROMOTE THE PEACEFUL USE OF NUCLEAR ENERGY.
THIS MADE THE U.S. GOVERNMENT SUSPICIOUS. IT WAS THE MIDDLE OF THE COLD WAR, WHEN PACIFISM WAS CONSIDERED DANGEROUS.
DON'T WALK
F.BEE-1
THE POLICE PUT HIM UNDER SURVEILLANCE.
AND WHEN HE STARTED DENOUNCING RACIAL SEGREGATION IN THE STATES, WHICH WAS DUE TO PREJUDICE AGAINST BLACK AMERICANS, THE HEAD OF THE FBI CALLED HIM AN "ENEMY OF THE STATE."
COMMUNIST
AGITATOR
AFTER ESCAPING TO AMERICA BECAUSE OF HIS RELIGION, HE WAS NOW OUTLAWED BECAUSE OF HIS IDEAS.
IT SURE ISN'T EASY BEING A GENIUS...

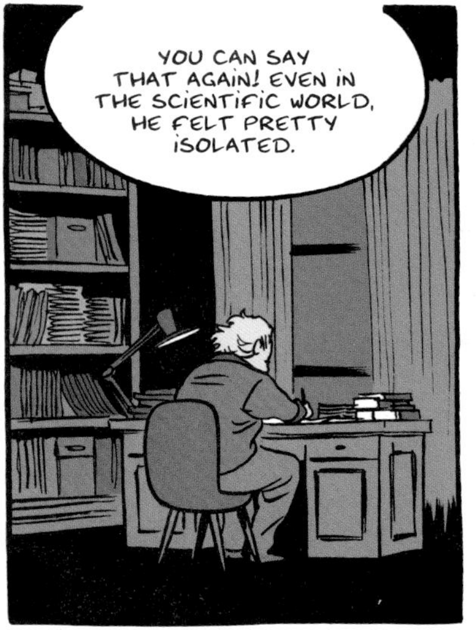
YOU CAN SAY THAT AGAIN! EVEN IN THE SCIENTIFIC WORLD, HE FELT PRETTY ISOLATED.

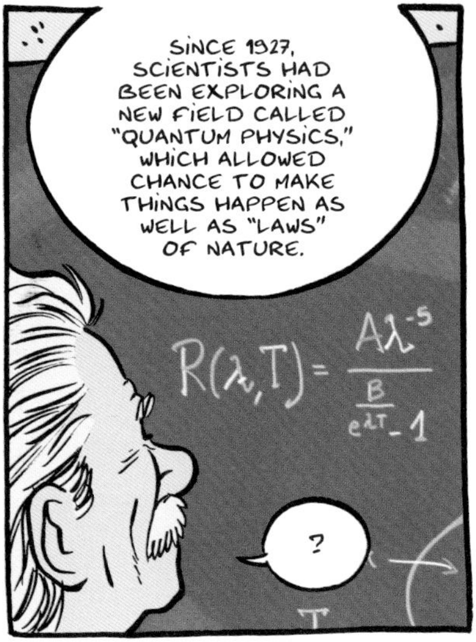
SINCE 1927, SCIENTISTS HAD BEEN EXPLORING A NEW FIELD CALLED "QUANTUM PHYSICS," WHICH ALLOWED CHANCE TO MAKE THINGS HAPPEN AS WELL AS "LAWS" OF NATURE.
R(λ,T) = Aλ^-5 / (B / e^λT - 1)
?

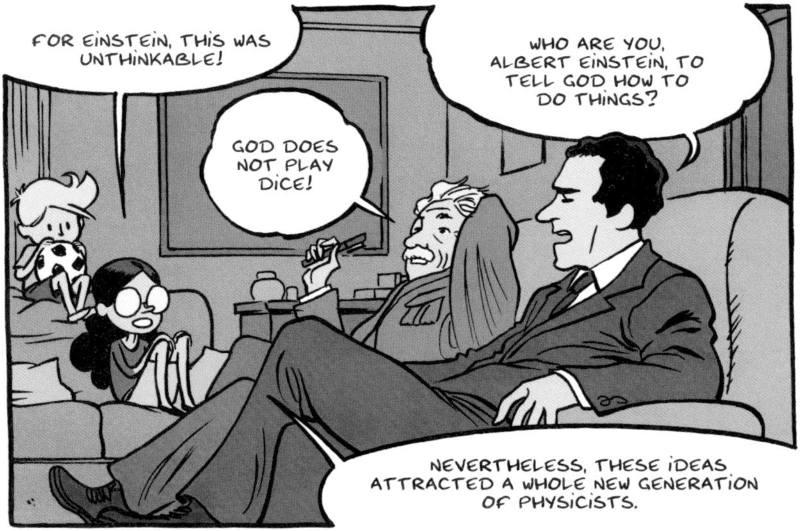
FOR EINSTEIN, THIS WAS UNTHINKABLE!
GOD DOES NOT PLAY DICE!
WHO ARE YOU, ALBERT EINSTEIN, TO TELL GOD HOW TO DO THINGS?
NEVERTHELESS, THESE IDEAS ATTRACTED A WHOLE NEW GENERATION OF PHYSICISTS.

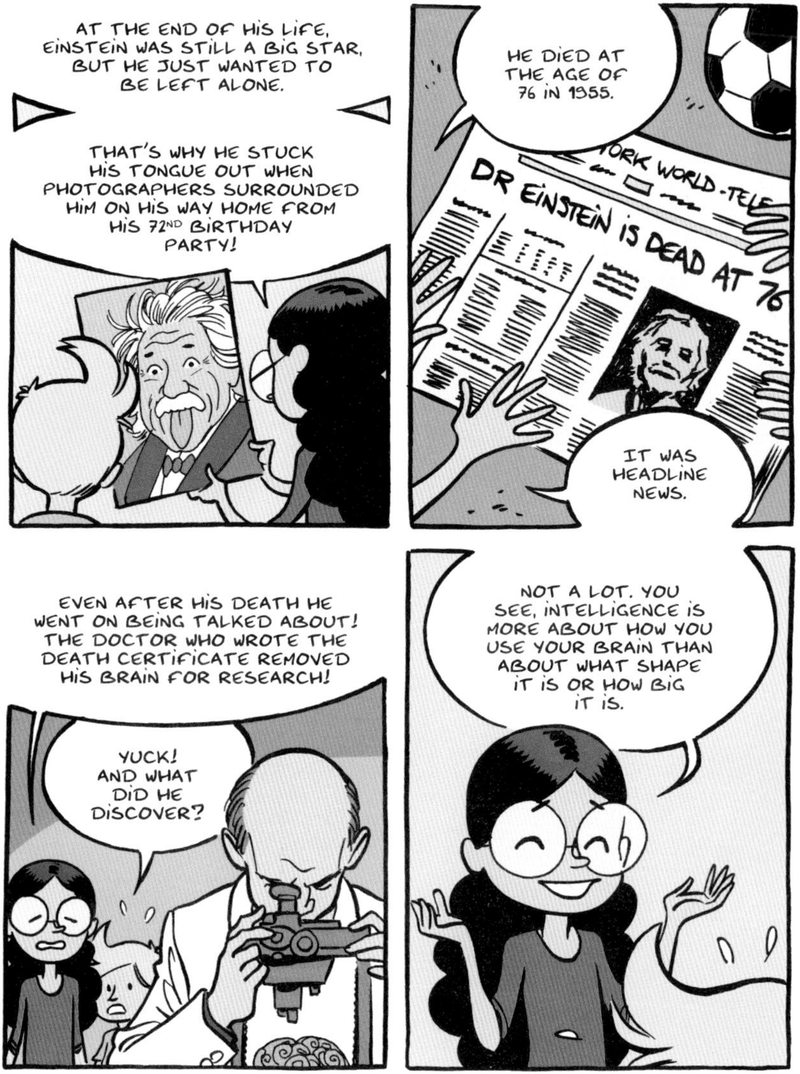
AT THE END OF HIS LIFE, EINSTEIN WAS STILL A BIG STAR, BUT HE JUST WANTED TO BE LEFT ALONE.
THAT'S WHY HE STUCK HIS TONGUE OUT WHEN PHOTOGRAPHERS SURROUNDED HIM ON HIS WAY HOME FROM HIS 72ND BIRTHDAY PARTY!
HE DIED AT THE AGE OF 76 IN 1955.
DR EINSTEIN IS DEAD AT 76
IT WAS HEADLINE NEWS.
EVEN AFTER HIS DEATH HE WENT ON BEING TALKED ABOUT! THE DOCTOR WHO WROTE THE DEATH CERTIFICATE REMOVED HIS BRAIN FOR RESEARCH!
YUCK! AND WHAT DID HE DISCOVER?
NOT A LOT. YOU SEE, INTELLIGENCE IS MORE ABOUT HOW YOU USE YOUR BRAIN THAN ABOUT WHAT SHAPE IT IS OR HOW BIG IT IS.

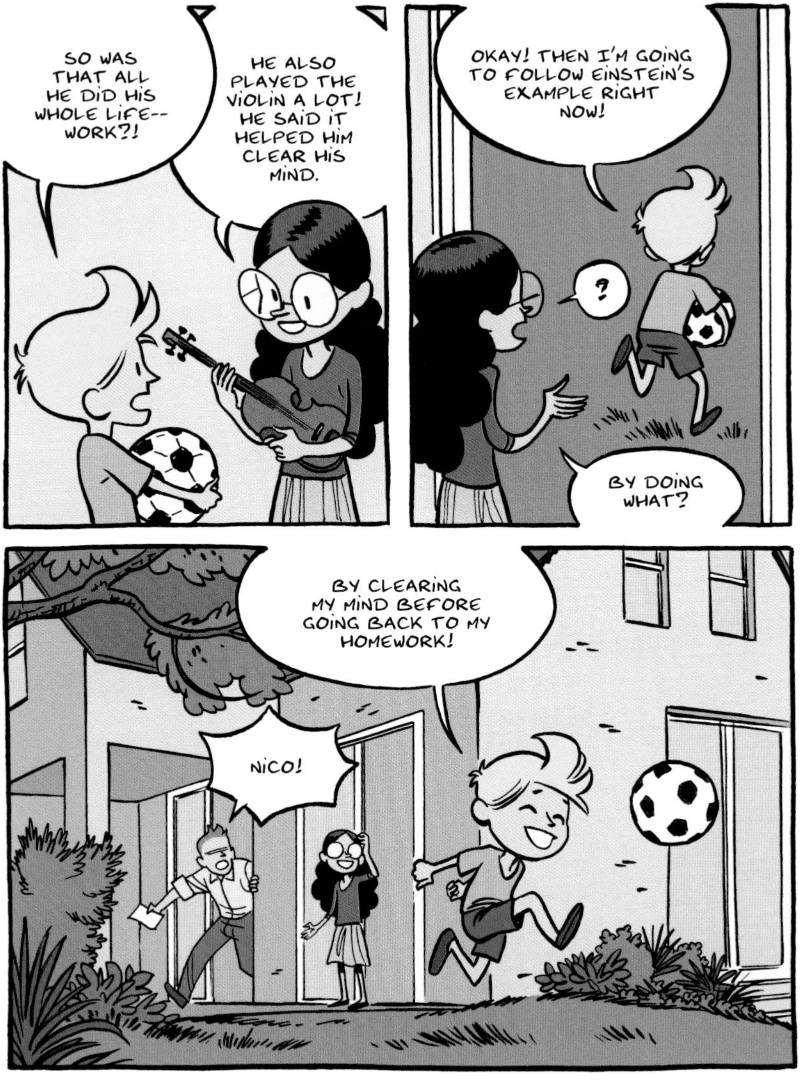
SO WAS THAT ALL HE DID HIS WHOLE LIFE-- WORK?!
HE ALSO PLAYED THE VIOLIN A LOT! HE SAID IT HELPED HIM CLEAR HIS MIND.
OKAY! THEN I'M GOING TO FOLLOW EINSTEIN'S EXAMPLE RIGHT NOW!
?
BY DOING WHAT?
BY CLEARING MY MIND BEFORE GOING BACK TO MY HOMEWORK!
NICO!

## And there's more...

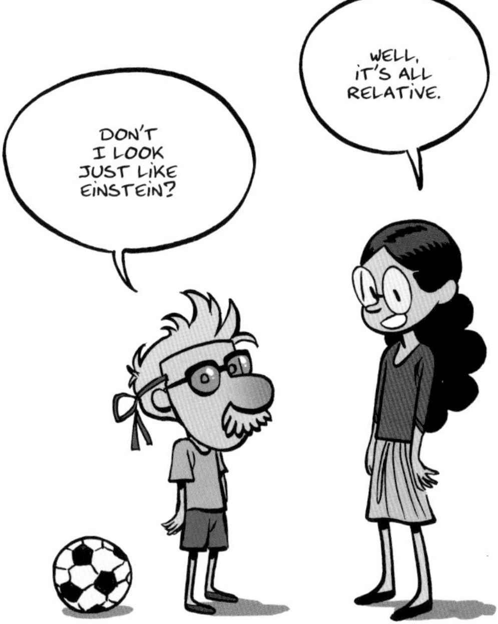
DON'T I LOOK JUST LIKE EINSTEIN?
WELL, IT'S ALL RELATIVE.

# Four other scientists who made history

## Max Planck
(1858-1947)

A German physicist who came up with the idea of particles (quanta), which Einstein later developed and which eventually led to quantum physics. It was Planck's observations that gave Einstein his ideas about light. Planck won the Nobel Prize in 1918 and was an early supporter of Einstein's theories. In 1929, he and Einstein won the very first Max Planck medals!

## Michele Besso
(1873-1955)

A Swiss physicist who first met Einstein when they were both at the Polytechnic Institute in Zurich and remained a close friend. Einstein's theories of relativity developed out of his long discussions with Besso, who was the only other person acknowledged in Einstein's 1905 articles. Besso also helped Albert and Mileva when they divorced, especially by looking after their children. He died in the same year as Einstein.

## Karl Schwarzschild
(1873-1916)

A German astrophysicist who was fighting on the Western Front when he read Einstein's paper on general relativity in November 1915. He immediately started making complicated calculations to work out how space-time curved around a star and demonstrated that there were black holes in space. He sent his findings to Einstein, who presented them on Schwarzschild's behalf to the Prussian Academy of Sciences.

## Robert Oppenheimer
(1904-1967)

An American physicist who was made scientific head of the Manhattan Project's weapons laboratory and worked on the atomic bomb. After the Second World War, he argued for the peaceful use of nuclear energy and was put under surveillance by the U.S. government. He then went back into research and served as Director of Princeton's Institute for Advanced Study, after Einstein.

# Was Mileva Marić overshadowed by Einstein?

How much credit should **Einstein's first wife** take for the development of his theories?

Einstein met Mileva Marić in 1896 at the Polytechnic Institute in Zurich. At that time, it was very rare for women to have access to higher education. Mileva's father had to get special permission for her to take courses normally reserved for men. She proved herself **highly gifted at both physics and math**, but became pregnant in 1900 and was unable to finish her studies, which made it difficult for her to pursue a career as a scientist.

Mileva and Albert married in 1903. They had three children together and for many years they lived as both **professional colleagues** and husband and wife, sharing ideas and discussing the theory of relativity. In a letter to Mileva, Albert even referred to it as "our theory."

But Mileva was restricted by convention, which expected her to be a housewife, and was never able to pursue a career as a researcher. Only Albert's name appeared on the articles that were published.

The marriage ended in divorce in 1919 and their relationship became strained. Albert distanced himself from her and even from their children, and **he would never acknowledge the part she claimed to have played** during their years of study and research.

So what was Mileva's contribution to Einstein's discoveries? **The question is still hotly debated.** For some, the fact that Albert continued to publish articles after their separation, while Mileva did not, proves that she was not involved in the development of the theories of relativity. For others, Mileva simply suffered the fate of many women at that time—to be forced to live and work in the shadow of men, without ever being given due recognition.

# Einstein and astronomy

## Eddington's observations

In May 1919, the English astrophysicist **Arthur Eddington** sailed to the islands of São Tomé and Principe, off the coast of Africa, to observe an eclipse of the sun. When the sun disappeared behind the moon, he saw that stars near to the sun appeared to be out of position relative to the Earth. **The light the stars emitted was deflected by the mass of the sun.** It proved that Einstein was right: space-time curved around a large mass.

APPARENT POSITION OF THE OBJECT
DISPLACEMENT OF THE IMAGE
ACTUAL POSITION OF THE OBJECT
MASS CAUSING THE DEFLECTION (E.G. THE SUN)
EARTH


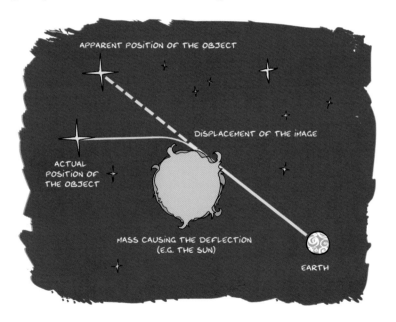

This phenomenon has been observed many times since. It is called "gravitational lensing" and it means that stars are not always where you think they are!

## Hubble's discovery

In 1929, the American astrophysicist **Edwin Hubble** argued that the universe is expanding—**the galaxies are getting farther and farther apart**. Einstein rejected this idea. He was convinced the universe was constant. Yet his own theories showed that it was expanding. So he tried to come up with formulas that would prove the theory wrong. He couldn't. Eventually, Einstein accepted the idea, and admitted that rejecting it had been "the stupidest mistake I ever made."

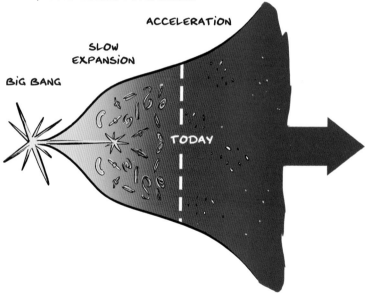

ACCELERATION
SLOW EXPANSION
BIG BANG
TODAY

Hubble's discovery eventually led to the **Big Bang theory**, according to which the universe started expanding 13.7 billion years ago.

# What use are Einstein's theories?

## They tell you where you are

GPS satellites that send the signals to our cars so we know where we are travel very fast through space as they orbit the Earth—which means that time passes more slowly for a satellite than it does for us, as Einstein predicted. So their built-in clocks have to be constantly adjusted for them to give us the right information.

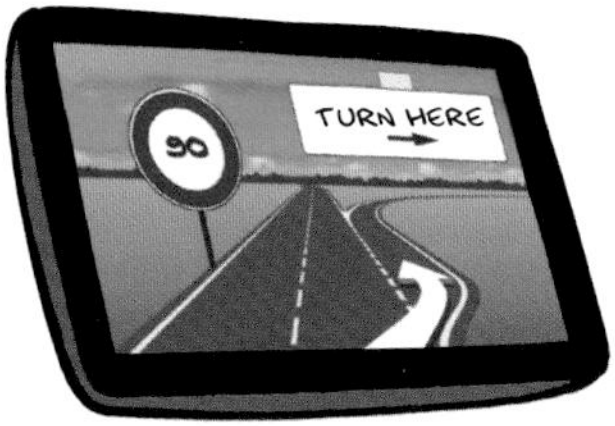
90
TURN HERE

## They make electric gates work

The "photoelectric effect" discovered by Einstein in 1905, which won him the 1921 Nobel Prize, means that light can generate an electric current. When we break the beam of light emitted by a gate, it opens automatically.

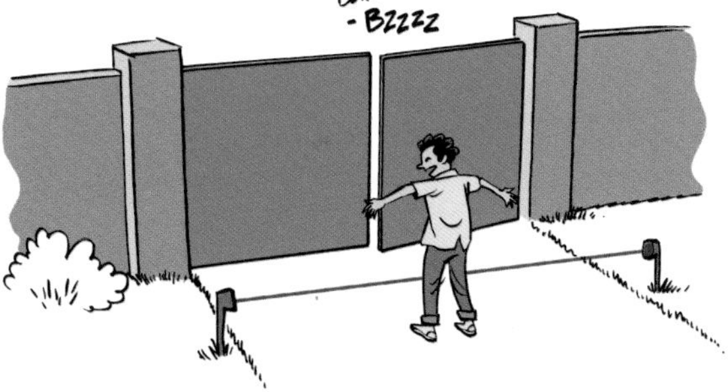
BLIP
- BZZZZ

## They generate electricity

Nuclear power stations work according to Einstein's famous formula, $E=mc^2$. When uranium is "burned," it releases a huge amount of heat, which can be used to generate electricity. But the process must be carefully controlled, or it could be disastrous!

## They help you to earn money (sometimes)

Decisions on how to invest in the stock market are based on Einstein's theory of "Brownian motion." But the laws of economics are not quite as precise as the laws of physics, which means that things don't always work out as they should. That's why there was a financial crash in 2008!

# Timeline

**Born in Ulm (Germany) on March 14th.**
▼

**Admitted to the Polytechnic Institute in Zurich (Switzerland).**
▼

**1879**

**1896**

**1933**

**1928**

▲
**Leaves Germany for good when Hitler comes to power.**

▲
**Becomes President of the International League for the Rights of Man.**

**1939**

**1948**

▲
**Writes to Franklin D. Roosevelt warning him of the danger of nuclear fission.**

▲
**Publishes his book _The World as I See It._**

"Annus mirabilis": publishes a series of groundbreaking articles that form the basis of the Theory of Special Relativity.

▼

**1905**

Finalizes the Theory of General Relativity.

▼

**1915**

**1925**

▲

Co-founds the Hebrew University of Jerusalem with, among others, Sigmund Freud.

**1921**

▲

Receives the Nobel Prize in Physics.

**1952**

▲

Refuses appointment as President of the State of Israel.

**1955**

▲

Dies in Princeton, New Jersey on April 18th.

43

# WATCH OUT FOR PAPERCUTZ

Welcome to the scientifically sensational sixth MAGICAL HISTORY TOUR graphic novel, this one focused on "Albert Einstein" painstakingly researched and written by Fabrice Erre and lavishly illustrated by Sylvain Savoia, from Papercutz, those science nerds dedicated to publishing great graphic novels for all ages. I'm Jim Salicrup, the Editor-in-Chief and Mad Genius here to talk a little about Albert Einstein…

I don't remember when I first saw Albert Einstein on television, but I instantly thought the man was a genius—a comedy genius. I never missed an appearance of his on the late-night talk shows as I knew they would always be inventively funny and totally hysterical. While Albert has appeared in many movies, having even written, directed, and starred in a few, he's probably best know to millions as the voice of Marlin in *Finding Nemo* and *Finding Dory*.

Hold on, I've just been informed by Managing Editor Jeff Whitman that this volume is actually about Albert Einstein the genius physicist, not the comedy genius born Albert Einstein who changed his name to Albert Brooks. Oops. Well, what's left for me to say about that Albert Einstein that isn't already covered in the rest of this graphic novel? Let me instead share some quotations from Albert Einstein himself, the genius physicist one, with my simple-minded responses…

*"If you can't explain it to a six-year old, you don't understand it yourself."*
        That could be the guiding principle behind this graphic novel series.
    *"If you want your children to be intelligent, read them fairy tales. If you want them to be more intelligent, read them more fairy tales."*
        Or comics!
  *"Logic will get you from A to Z; imagination will get you everywhere."*
        Yet, it was Daffy Duck who once sang, "You never know where you're
        going until you get there."
*"Life is like riding a bicycle. To keep your balance, you must keep moving."*
        Moving right along…

*"Never memorize something that you can look up."*

I've always thought that! Guess great minds do think alike!

*"Reality is merely an illusion, albeit a very persistent one."*

But is illusion reality?

*"The important thing is not to stop questioning. Curiosity has its own reason for existence. One cannot help but be in awe when he contemplates the mysteries of eternity, of life, of the marvelous structure of reality. It is enough if one tries merely to comprehend a little of this mystery each day."*

Yeah, but look what happened to the poor curious cat!

*"Time is an illusion."*

Tell that to Jeff Whitman, Managing Editor, when one our books is late

*"I'd rather be an optimist and a fool than a pessimist and right."*

Words I live by!

Gee, that was fun. It's not often I get to chat with a certified genius. As a result, I'm now approaching the end of this column a little bit differently than usual. Instead of saying that the next volume of MAGICAL HISTORY TOUR is "coming soon" like I usually do, I now realize more fully that time is truly relative. Kind of an ironic revelation to have in a book where the main characters travel through time! But now I'm aware that you may be reading these words many years after this book was originally published, so the next volume isn't "coming soon," it was already published years ago. So, let me put it this way, at some point in time, MAGICAL HISTORY TOUR Volume Seven will be released, and if you've enjoyed this volume, or any other volume of MAGICAL HISTORY TOUR, I suspect you'll enjoy Volume Seven too! There — I hope Albert Einstein would approve of that!

Thank you,

## STAY IN TOUCH!

| | |
|---|---|
| EMAIL: | salicrup@papercutz.com |
| WEB: | www.papercutz.com |
| TWITTER: | @papercutzgn |
| INSTAGRAM: | @papercutzgn |
| FACEBOOK: | PAPERCUTZGRAPHICNOVELS |
| FANMAIL: | Papercutz, 160 Broadway, Suite 700, East Wing, New York, NY 10038 |

Go to papercutz.com and sign up for the free Papercutz e-newsletter!

**Fabrice Erre** has a Ph.D. in History and teaches Geography and History at the Lycee Jean Jaures near Montpellier, France. He has written a thesis on the satirical press, writes the blog *Une annee au lycee (A Year in High School)* on the website of *Le Monde*, one of France's top national newspapers, and has published several comics.

**Sylvain Savoia** draws the *Marzi* series, which tells the history of Poland as seen through the eyes of a child. He has also drawn *Les esclaves oublies de Tromelin (The Forgotten Slaves of Tromelin)*, which won the *Academie de Marine de Paris* prize.

# MORE GREAT GRAPHIC NOVEL SERIES AVAILABLE FROM PAPERCUTZ™

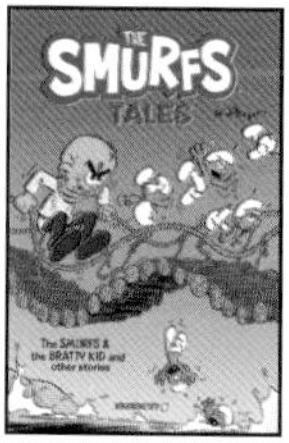
THE SMURFS TALES
The SMURFS & the BRATTY KID and other stories
THE SMURFS TALES

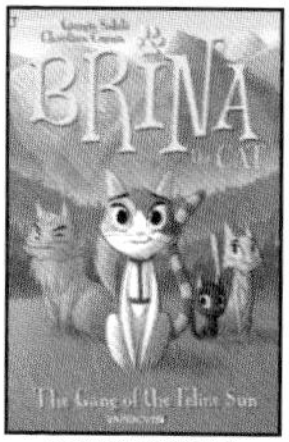
BRINA
The Gang of the Feline Sun
BRINA THE CAT

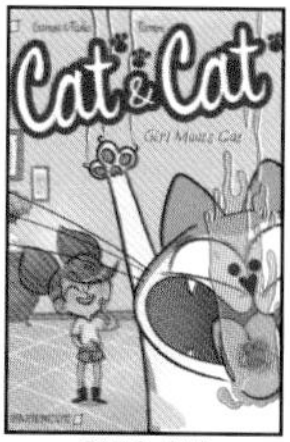
Cat & Cat
Girl Meets Cat
CAT & CAT

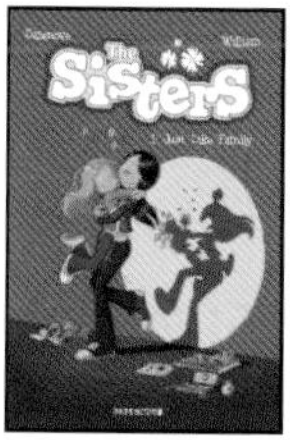
The Sisters
THE SISTERS

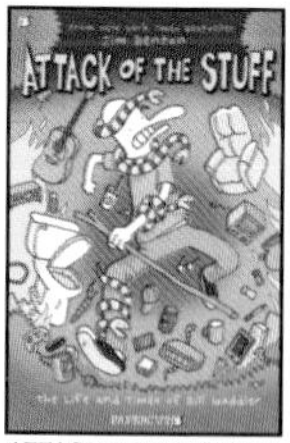
ATTACK OF THE STUFF
ATTACK OF THE STUFF

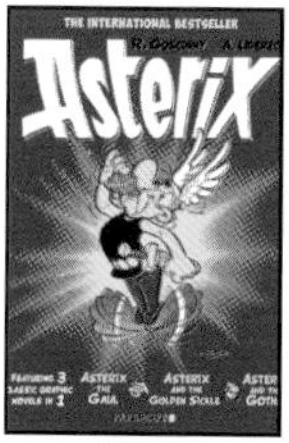
THE INTERNATIONAL BESTSELLER
Asterix
ASTERIX

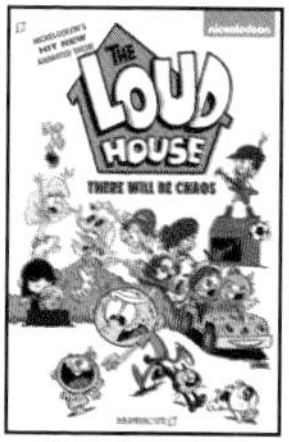
THE LOUD HOUSE
THERE WILL BE CHAOS
THE LOUD HOUSE

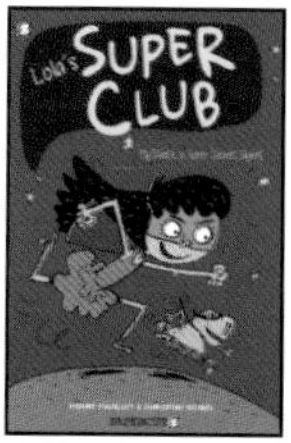
Lola's SUPER CLUB
LOLA'S SUPER CLUB

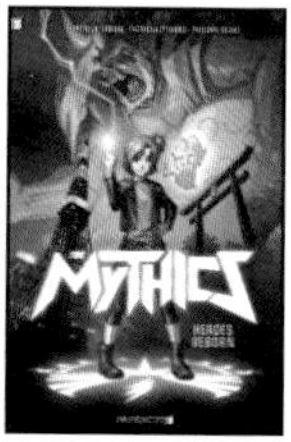
MYTHICS
HEROES REBORN
THE MYTHICS

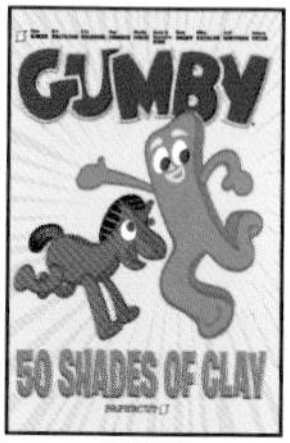
GUMBY
50 SHADES OF CLAY
GUMBY

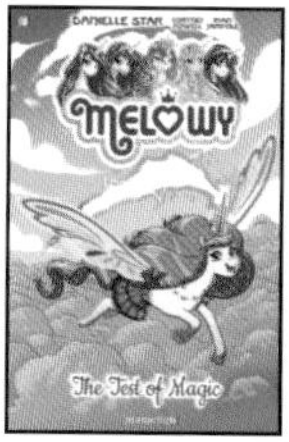
MELOWY
The Test of Magic
MELOWY

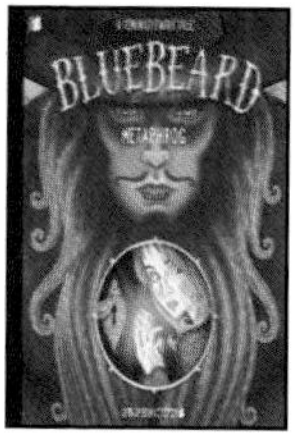
BLUEBEARD
BLUEBEARD

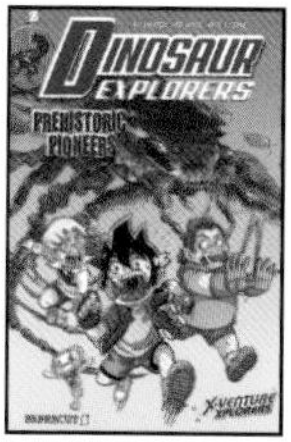
DINOSAUR EXPLORERS
PREHISTORIC PIONEERS
DINOSAUR EXPLORERS

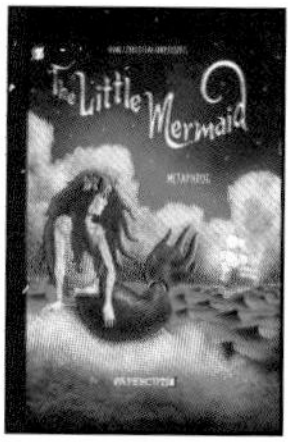
The Little Mermaid
THE LITTLE MERMAID

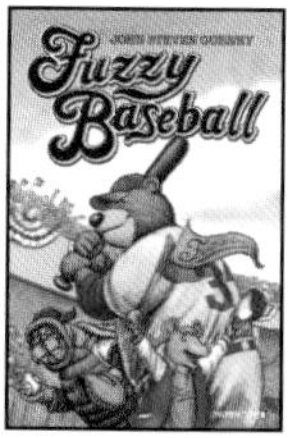
Fuzzy Baseball
FUZZY BASEBALL

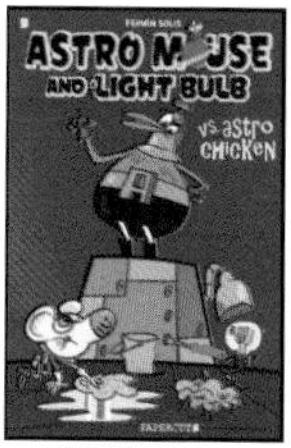
ASTRO MOUSE AND LIGHT BULB
vs. astro CHICKEN
ASTRO MOUSE AND LIGHT BULB

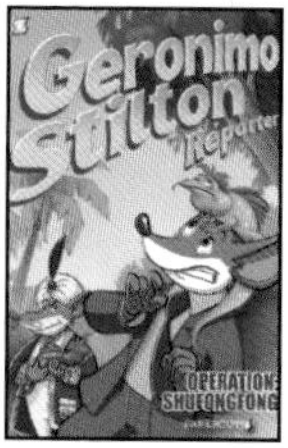
Geronimo Stilton Reporter
OPERATION SHUFONGFONG
GERONIMO STILTON REPORTER

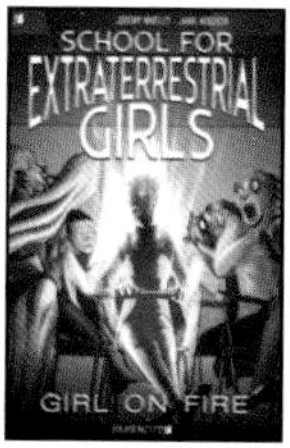
SCHOOL FOR EXTRATERRESTRIAL GIRLS
GIRL ON FIRE
SCHOOL FOR EXTRA-TERRESTRIAL GIRLS

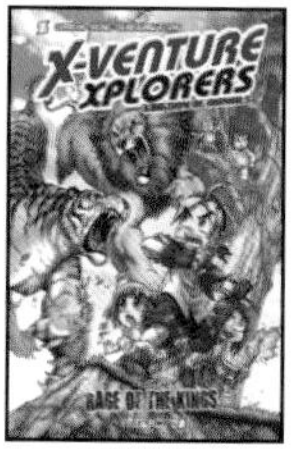
X-VENTURE XPLORERS
X-VENTURE XPLORERS

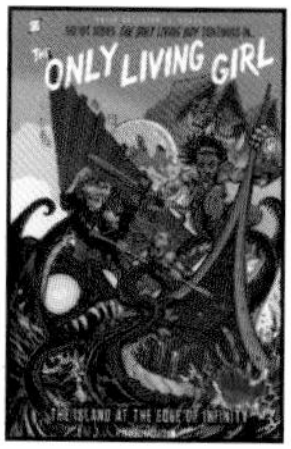
THE ONLY LIVING GIRL
THE ONLY LIVING GIRL

**papercutz.com**

Also available where ebooks are sold.

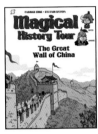